5 REASONS TO LOVE THIS BOOK...

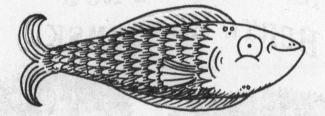

 It's so funny you will patoof yourself!

 Perfect for fans of David Walliams and Andy Stanton

 Chock-full of **CRAZLEPOPS** characters

 You'll be cheerzing like a nutcracker for Berto, Zoltan, and Tom!

Includes amazing extras—learn how to make a goat-hair moustache!

WISE WORDS FROM BERTO BABOOMSKI

When life gives you patonkleberries, make hot chocolate.

You can only fail if you don't try.

Never forget to remember who you is.

Even when you soar like eagle, you can still land in a pile of pootle. This is life. But it don't stop you trying to fly.

Walk tall!
Kiss the stars, lick the moon!

Don't smell the fear—it stinks! Sniff with your mind!

The truth is at the bottom of your heart; the power is at the heart of your bottom!

Open your mind, shut your face!

Sometimes a big pile of pootle can grow a beautiful flower.

In life, doings things is easy, doing the right thing is hard.

Good friends is like happiness: too much is never enough.

Mr. BABOOMSKI
and the
WONDER
GOAT

RICHARD JOYCE

Illustrated by Freya Hartas

OXFORD
UNIVERSITY PRESS

For Anna, Tom, and Sylvie
with all my love

OXFORD
UNIVERSITY PRESS

Great Clarendon Street, Oxford OX2 6DP
Oxford University Press is a department of the University of Oxford.
It furthers the University's objective of excellence in research, scholarship,
and education by publishing worldwide. Oxford is a registered trade mark
of Oxford University Press in the UK and in certain other countries

Copyright © Richard Joyce 2016
Illustrations © Freya Hartas 2016

The moral rights of the author have been asserted

Database right Oxford University Press (maker)

First published 2016

British Library Cataloguing in Publication Data

Data available

ISBN: 978-0-19-274460-9

1 3 5 7 9 10 8 6 4 2

Printed in Great Britain

Paper used in the production of this book is a natural,
recyclable product made from wood grown in sustainable forests.
The manufacturing process conforms to the environmental
regulations of the country of origin.

❧ CONTENTS ❧

CLIFFHANGER

I guess you never really know how great something is until it's gone. There's a verse in a song by my dad's favourite singer, Throaty Malone, which sums this up really well:

> **I cried like a babe when my dog
> left town,
> I got real blue when I stepped in
> something brown.
> When that mutt was around, I
> couldn't care less,
> Now that he's gone, my life is such
> a mess.**

As I wipe my trainer on a tuft of grass at the side of the path I find myself humming the first few lines of 'Dog Gone Blues', wishing that I could get my old life back. The wind howls in from the sea dragging gulls screeching over my

head. Far in the distance, across the fields, the sight of a twinkling light sends my heart sliding slowly down my trouser leg. The wind gets stronger, spitting rain in my face. I'm desperate to run home but that's not an option. I lean against the rusty chain marking the edge of the cliff; looking down between my feet as I swing forward, I can see frothy waves smashing into the dark rocks far below. If my parents could see me now, they would have a fit, but they can't see me—Mum's on the other side of the world and Dad's stuck in a cupboard, reeking of stale fish. Why did we have to come and live here? I was perfectly happy with things as they were: our old house, my old school. Now everything's changed. Mum's not around, Dad's miserable, my new school stinks and right now, just to cap it all, I've got to walk across a boggy field in a howling gale and tell a complete and utter nutcake that I accidentally murdered his flipping goat.

I suppose I'd better explain.

BOOM! BOOM!

The tiny kitchen was full of smoke, and the blues. Dad emerged through the fog looking grim and plonked a plate onto the table. I peered down at the six black rectangles covered in white blobs. Dominoes?

'Fish fingers drizzled in mayo. Eat up—you don't want to be late for school on your first day.'

He disappeared back into the smog and cranked up the stereo, Throaty howled out the opening bars of 'Moody Morning':

**The sun comes up, ol' blackbird
starts to sing,
A sweet, lonesome tale of life
upon the wing.
I lie in bed and my heart fills
with sorrow,
I reach for my rifle–he won't be
there tomorrow.**

I spotted a mean-looking seagull peering at me through the rain-lashed window, its beady eye trained on my charred breakfast. When I prodded a fish finger with my fork, it shattered into sooty shards. With an angry squawk the gull flapped off into the lead-grey sky. I pushed my plate away and reached for the postcard sitting on the grimy table. On one side there was a donkey in a straw hat standing under a palm tree grinning like an idiot. On the other, ten words:

'Special Project going well. Back soon. Love you loads! Mum.'

Mum was in Questimu, a small island off the coast of South America, home to the Pear-Shaped Planet Foundation, a charity run by Dr Smoothy: a fruit-loving rock star on a mission to save the world. (Dad used to be his biggest fan; lately he's been more into the blues.)

Mum had been chosen to lead a project using wind power to create affordable energy for poor communities—after years of sitting behind a desk in the London office this was her big break. 'I've got to do this, Tom,' she whispered tearfully at the airport. 'I shouldn't

12

be gone long—you guys will be fine. I mean, what's the worst that can happen?'

A week later, down a crackly phone line, I let her know.

'He's what?'

'Lost his job—slept through the alarm five days running. He's sitting in his underwear on the kitchen floor eating cold baked beans out of a flowerpot. How's the wind farm going?'

There was a mournful rasp from the kitchen.

Mum sighed. 'Not as well as yours by the sound of it. Listen, Tom, give Uncle Pete a call—there's always work going at his place and the sea air will do you both good.'

So here I was, somewhere in the depths of Cornwall on a rainy, moody Monday morning. Trudging along the damp high street I got my first proper look at Trefuggle Bay. It was, in a word, scubblyish. Scubbly is the name of the fish they are famous for in Trefuggle Bay. There was the Scubbly Museum, the Lucky Scubbly bingo hall, the Bubbly Scubbly launderette;

even the pub was called the Jolly Scubbly.
At the edge of the bay a palatial restaurant
called the Golden Scubbly gazed out to sea;
tethered to its tallest turret, a vast inflatable
fish dipped and bobbed in the stiff sea breeze.

Like everything else in town there was
something fishy about the school. As I walked
through the gates the headmistress, Mrs Pudyn,
pounced, spewing out words in a dribbling
mess of lisps and hisses.

'You must be Tom Watkinssss. Welcome to
Sssssaint Ssscubbly'ssss,' she hisped.

I dabbed the spit from my eyebrows and
looked up at the sign above the school gates. A
fish wearing a halo gaped back.

A limousine purred up and a large, round
boy bounced out munching a toffee apple.
The Head hissed like a punctured tyre.

'Sssstop sssstuffing yourssself, Hubert!'

Hubert's mouth gaped open, and chunks of
sugary apple dribbled down his blazer. 'Duh,
OK, Mum.'

The Head glowered at him. 'We are in
sssschool now.'

'Oh yeah, sorry, Mum, I mean Miss,' he
replied dozily.

Another posh car drew up; a uniformed chauffeur ushered out another boy: he had a pair of MegaSonic headphones clamped over his ears, his darting, beady eyes were fixed on a Pro-edition Gamestation.

'Good morning, Piersss,' Mrs Pudyn drooled.

He ignored her and wandered to the far corner of the playground where Hubert was dangling a pair of liquorice laces into his gaping mouth.

After the noise of the playground, the classroom was eerily quiet. I took a seat near the back and watched my new classmates cluster nervously in a corner, whispering amongst themselves. The volume rose when Piers and Hubert arrived. They stomped around, flicking ears and tugging ponytails, cackling like hyenas. When Piers spotted me, he gave an oily smirk then strode over to my desk and leaned forward until his sharp beak was only inches from my face. A deathly hush fell over the classroom. His eyes narrowed into knife slits as he spat out three poison-drenched words:

'HOW DARE YOU!'

How dare who? I looked around the classroom, mystified. The other kids were studying the floor.

'That's my place. I am Piers Smerkinton-Peck and no one sits down until I do—it's the rule.'

Rule? Hubert came and stood by his side, grinning dopily through a gluey rainbow of wine gums. Oh well, I didn't want any trouble on my first day. I picked up my stuff and headed for another desk, tripped over Piers's outstretched foot and fell sprawling to the floor. Hubert guffawed, spraying fountains of wine-gummy spit into the air.

Piers spent ages spreading a huge stash of fancy stationery across his desk then produced a velvet cushion from his bag which he placed on his chair. Finally, with a triumphant smirk around the room, he sat down. The other kids shuffled silently to their places.

I couldn't believe my eyes—who did this little squit think he was? I was hoping the teacher would put him in his place, but one look at Miss Thompson told me I was out of luck. She scuttled into the room, peering nervously through the narrow gap between the top of her glasses and the bottom of her sharp fringe.

While the rest of the class got on with their work, Piers lounged on his cushion, peering down at the Gamestation on his lap, occasionally passing Hubert a bag of sweets or bar of chocolate. Basically he was paying the great lump to be his bodyguard. You might have thought all that sugar would have made Hubert a bundle of energy but the opposite was true—when he wasn't feeding his face, he slept, his great, raking snores drowning out Miss Thompson's quivering voice.

I was already missing the teacher from my old school: Miss Akira. She was tiny and softly-spoken and the class loudmouth, Desmond Larkins, had tried his luck on day one. She asked him to settle down. He ignored her. She asked him again. No response. In a flash Miss Akira zipped over to his desk and pinched his earlobe between her thumb and forefinger.

'EEEEEEH!' Desmond squealed like a scalded piglet taking a corner too fast. 'Miss! What are you doing?'

'It's called the joyless crab,' she replied, softly, 'and these'—she hooked her fingers under his nostrils and yanked them backwards—'are the tunnels of despair.' Desmond yelped for mercy. Miss Akira released him, gave a little bow, and scooted back to her desk. We learnt loads that term about Buddhism and Zen philosophies. Most of all we learnt that you should never, under any circumstances, mess with Miss Akira.

I watched Piers wriggling on his cushion, hunched over his Gamestation and wished someone could put him in his place. Suddenly I had a great idea. And by 'great' I mean pretty terrible.

After lunch I slipped out of the playground and legged it back to the tiny cottage Uncle Pete had found for us to stay in. I grabbed my rucksack and rummaged through the few precious items I had brought from home. I opened a small, metal tin and tipped the contents into my hand. What lay there looked like tiny rugby balls, each with a little stalk. Bangers, killer bangers: Thunder Bombs! I placed them carefully in the inside pocket of my blazer and ran back to school.

I snuck into the classroom, slid a Thunder Bomb under Piers's special cushion, and was about to add the second when I heard voices. I slipped it into my pocket and sauntered to the back of the room. Piers was the last to arrive. I held my breath. After what seemed like years, he cast a snotty glance around the room and then, finally, sat down.

But not for long . . .

BOOM!!!

The explosion was supersonic: the walls shook, the floorboards shuddered. Piers squeaked like an electrified mouse and leapt into a star jump, booting over the desk, scattering his precious stationery collection across the floor. As he rose, one of his windmilling arms caught Hubert under his chins. He fell backwards over a desk, while the jumbo sack of cheddar puffs he had been grazing on spun through the air showering him in cheesy confetti. A snort of laughter exploded from my nose.

'Get him!' snarled Piers.

Hubert lumbered towards me trying to look menacing—not easy when you've got a generous handful of cheddar puffs in your hair. I tried to sidestep his lunge but he caught me in a tight headlock. We staggered forward like a wild, four-legged beast, collapsing onto Piers who was still on his knees collecting his pens. He squealed, like the last squeak of air escaping a runaway balloon. A few seconds of silence followed. Then I heard an angry hiss.

Mrs Pudyn was standing in the doorway, foaming at the mouth, bulleting frothy spitballs halfway across the classroom.

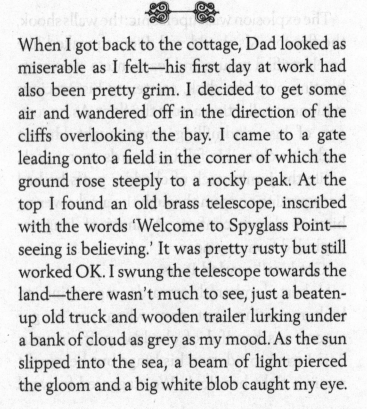

When I got back to the cottage, Dad looked as miserable as I felt—his first day at work had also been pretty grim. I decided to get some air and wandered off in the direction of the cliffs overlooking the bay. I came to a gate leading onto a field in the corner of which the ground rose steeply to a rocky peak. At the top I found an old brass telescope, inscribed with the words 'Welcome to Spyglass Point— seeing is believing.' It was pretty rusty but still worked OK. I swung the telescope towards the land—there wasn't much to see, just a beaten-up old truck and wooden trailer lurking under a bank of cloud as grey as my mood. As the sun slipped into the sea, a beam of light pierced the gloom and a big white blob caught my eye.

At first I thought it was a chunk of chalky rock but it was moving, drifting slowly up the field towards me.

It was a goat, a flipping massive goat.

I clambered down from Spyglass Point. The goat ambled up and stopped, head on one side, munching a stalk of grass, gazing at me with dreamy-looking eyes the colour of liquid honey. Suddenly it lunged forward, butting me in the stomach.

'Oi!' I shouted.

The goat lunged again, shoving its shaggy head under my chin, slapping me round the chops with its long, rasping tongue. It was unbearably ticklish in a gross sort of way. Soon I was giggling helplessly; my black mood had lifted. I reached out a hand and stroked the goat's soft, pink nose.

'Thanks for that.'

It gazed back dozily and lowered a sleepy eyelid. Then it stuck its head down the front of my school jumper.

'Whoa!' I staggered backwards.

The goat hopped back, still chewing. Only this time, instead of grass-slurping, I heard the crunch of a cheddar puff. It must have slipped out of Hubert's hair and fallen down the front of my jumper during the fight. The shaggy beast came back for more and started nosing around inside my blazer, nudging me in the ribs. I was laughing so much I could hardly think straight—what's in there? Maybe it's an old sweet or . . .

My ears rang, smoke danced before my eyes. At first I thought the goat had run off but then

I looked down and saw a sight that turned my blood to ice. It was lying at my feet, tongue lolling out, legs sticking up like flagpoles.

A noise in the far distance woke me up. Across the field I could see a man emerging from the old trailer, shouting in my direction and shaking his fist.

I shifted faster than Hubert on roller skates heading downhill to an all-you-can-eat buffet.

A CRAZY-LOOKING NUTCAKE WITH A BONKERS MOUSTACHE

Doing the right thing is never easy.

One of Mum's favourite expressions kept running through my head as I dawdled along the clifftop path early the next morning after a sleepless night. The right thing to do was to own up about the banger and the goat but who should I tell? There was no farmhouse to be seen anywhere up on the cliffs; I'd have to try the man in the trailer. As I neared the gate to the fields, I peered over at the crime scene but there was nothing to see. A gull screeched eerily overhead. They must have already disposed of the body.

I was so busy looking for goat corpses that I wasn't watching my step. Suddenly my foot shot forward, skiing through a coil of fresh dog poo. Could life get any worse? It started to rain. OK, now could life get any worse? It started to hail. Lightning crackled overhead, thunder boomed. I started running across the field towards the trailer—I was soon out of control, feet skating on the slimy mud, arms windmilling. I had planned to knock politely on the door. BANG! I slammed into the side of the trailer with a noise that made the gulls half a mile out to sea shriek in panic, and then fell backwards into a muddy puddle. The door of the trailer creaked open. Through the driving rain I saw the outline of a large figure standing in the doorway. Suddenly a fork of lightning speared into the lead-grey sea.

In that split second of light I saw enough to convince me that I had done the wrong thing.

I was staring up at a wild-looking man with curtains of black hair straggling either side of a crooked top hat, mad, staring eyes, and a deranged, gap-toothed grin peering out of a huge, twirling moustache. He bent down, grabbed my collar, and hauled me into the trailer, slamming the door behind him. I

stumbled into the darkness and collapsed onto a pile of old blankets. I was shaking like mad, partly because of the chill from my wet clothes and partly because I was trapped in the middle of nowhere with a crazy-looking nutcake with a bonkers moustache. I tried to speak but my teeth were chattering too much.

He chucked a piece of wood on a stove. It flared up, giving me a slightly better view of my surroundings. The trailer was full of weird-looking junk jumbling all over the place but what really caught my eye was a faded photograph on the wall of the man and the goat. It was in a novelty frame bearing the words **Best Friends 4 Ever!** in bubble writing.

The man had his back to me. It was too gloomy to see what he was doing but when I heard the metallic clink of a blade being sharpened, I started shaking twice as hard. Time to get out of here; I'd confess about the goat some other time—write him a nice letter, perhaps an anonymous postcard? The windows were locked, rattling in the howling gale. I could make a run for the door but that meant nipping past the bloodthirsty psychopath humming cheerfully as he pottered around in the kitchen. I got slowly to my feet and began edging towards freedom.

Suddenly the man swung around and lunged towards me. As the fire leapt, I saw a long, silver dagger being thrust in my direction. I tried to scream but only managed a squeaky choke. I stared wide-eyed at the point of the blade a few inches from my nose. It stared back. It had eyes. It had a face. It was a fish. I looked up at the man.

'You hungry, boy?'

He dropped the fish into a pan on top of the stove then handed me a dented tin mug.

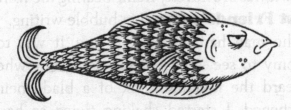

Eh? One minute I was being murdered, the next it was tea-time. I gripped the mug in my trembling hands and took a sip. The creamy hot chocolate slid down my throat, warming me to my toes. It was so tasty I accidentally let out a little 'Mmmm', forgetting that I was in mortal danger. The man shuffled over to the stove, picked up a thick slice of bread that had been toasting there, chucked the fish on top, and handed it to me.

'Here, boy, you eat.'

The fish on toast disappeared just as fast as the hot chocolate. I had never tasted anything like it: sweet, juicy, salty, lemony, coconutty—seriously, coconutty!—tangy, spicy . . . So many ways to describe that brilliant taste but my host summed it up in a single word.

'**SKABOONKY**?' he asked, patting his belly.

'It's great, thank you,' I spluttered with my mouth full.

He settled into his tatty armchair and began dunking his curly moustache into his hot chocolate. 'Mmm, **SKABOONKY**.'

He drained his mug, fumbled around in his ragged coat and pulled out a long thin pipe which he lit from the stove.

The fire was warming up my damp clothes and I had almost stopped shaking. I glanced across at the man puffing away quietly, gazing into the fire. He had looked a whole lot scarier a few minutes ago when I thought he was a knife-wielding maniac. But who was he?

I decided to come clean about the whole banger business and cleared my throat. The man looked up from the fire and took a long draw on his pipe. A crooked grin lifted the drooping curtains of his chocolate-soaked moustache; a snake of smoke curled through the gap between his front teeth.

'So, boy—you eat, you drink: you feel better now.'

'Yes, m-much better, th-thank you,' I stammered. 'But listen, I really need to explain what happened yesterday to your, erm, goat.'

He frowned but didn't say anything, so I carried on.

'You see, the thing is I played a trick on this boy at school—Piers, he's a complete nut job to be honest—and so I had this spare banger in my pocket—a Thunder Bomb . . . they're really loud . . . well, I guess you know that—and I forgot all about it and then your goat suddenly appeared and was sort of nosing around in my blazer, looking for food, and kind of butted me in the pocket and the banger went off and the goat got a big shock which I suppose was what maybe made it, you know, sort of, well, um . . . die. A bit.'

It took about ten seconds to blurt out that lot. I started off OK but as I got to the awkward (murdery) part of the story, the man started frowning. By the end my heart was thumping so hard it felt as though my corner of the trailer was rising and falling in time with my heavy breathing.

He placed his pipe on the stove, stood up, and walked over to where I was sitting. He bent down on his haunches and leaned forward so that his face was only a few inches from mine. His crooked teeth crawled out from beneath his moustache but he wasn't grinning now. I sat there, frozen to the spot. I couldn't meet his gaze so I focused instead on the space between his wonky front teeth. Suddenly two sharp, high-pitched whistles escaped from the gap like a train screaming out of a tunnel. And then I was down, rolling across the floor in a mess of arms, legs, and blankets. OK, here we go, I thought. This is it, he's going to finish me off. I couldn't bring myself to look; I just lay there on the floor curled into a ball, eyes screwed tightly shut.

Nothing happened. I opened one eye, then the other. **SPLOₒPSH!** I felt a long, sandpapery tongue slide across my forehead.

'Uuurgh! Gedoff! What the—'

Then I saw a pair of familiar-looking eyes staring down at me, dreamy-looking eyes the colour of liquid honey. The man chuckled, helped me to my feet, and ruffled my hair.

'Boy, meet Zoltan.'

I was too confused to speak. For a moment I wondered if the goat was really there. It gave me a friendly butt in the stomach. 'Oof!' It was there all right. The man held out a bony hand.

'I is Berto Socrates Baboomski. I comes from Escorvia. Pleased for meeting you.'

My head was spinning with questions.

'Escorvia? Where's that?'

'Not so far.'

'How did you end up here?'

'Long story.'

'How did you make the goat come back to life?'

'Even longerer story.'

The man gathered up the blankets and piled them in the corner of the trailer where the goat snuggled down under them. 'Have seat, boy.'

I sat on the blankets and leaned back against the goat. It felt like a warm, living sofa. Now I understood why it had seemed like the whole trailer had been moving. The man eased into his armchair, tossed another log onto the fire, collected his pipe from the top of the stove, and told me his story.

ZOLTAN, PEYPA

When I is small boy, the Baboomski family is famous; we is the kings of the circus. I travel all over Escorvia with my Pappy and Grandpappy. We have beautiful animals, angry bats swinging in the sky, and clowns running around like crazlepops, kicking each other in the **BABUNSKA**.

We travel together, all over the beautiful land of Escorvia. We catch fish, we pick frutas from the trees and salatas from the ground. Ah, **SKABOONKY!** We have big fire: we cook, we eat, we dance, we sing. Every day we come to new town or village.

They wait long time for this special day. Life is good, everybody happy.

Then one day, on a farm in north of Escorvia, a pig called Gyorgy climbs through hole in hedge and walks into field next door. He eats turnip. The turnip farmer gets mad and shoots Gyorgy. The piggy farmer gets mad and shoots the turnip farmer—

BANG!
—right in his **BABUNSKA**. Soon all farmers in north are trying to shoot each other in the **BABUNSKA**. This spreads like fire, until whole country is fighting itself. Five years this goes on. My Pappy

has to go back to our village to fight. Every day I look down road to see him come back. He never do. One day letter come with medal. Grandpappy washes it in tears then pins it on my shirt.

'I is old, Berto. Soon will be time for longest sleep. You is Mr Baboomski of circus now.'

'But I is not ready,' I say. 'I need more learnings.'

Grandpappy shakes his head. 'You was born ready for this, Berto Socrates Baboomski. The circus is in your blood and in your heart, but don't forget this—' he taps me gently on the noggin '—you is named Socrates for some clever thinkings. Use your nut and everything will be fine.

Now get packed. I need some snorings.'

So now I is Mr Baboomski of circus, but what is left to boss up? When war finish, Escorvia is changed: fields are black, forest is hushed up, mountains are full of ghosts. We tries to make a show but peoples don't come. They is too sad after war. Soon we have no money to feed animals; the angry bats and clowns go home to their villages. Before long it is only me and two clowns: Clonky and Clinky—they are mini-men, but they has big hearts. Life on road is gloomish, Escorvia is dead country: no more fish in river, the trees are all sticky.

We walks to market in the snow to sell our last horse, Plonki. Not much is for selling—everything is grey, peoples look sad. A man called O'Flanigan says he will buy Plonki, but he don't have enough money. 'Come with me,' he say. We walk to a field on the edge of market where two goats are nibbling the frosty grass. One is white like snow, the other is speckly grey.

'Twin girls,' says O'Flanigan. 'Zoltan, Peypa—you can't have one without the other!'

These goats is big and strong, maybe we have milk and cheese—is better than one hungry horse—so I agree to swap. Then a truck drives past and the tail-pipe goes off: **BANG!**

Goats fall down—I think they dead.

'Hey!' I say to O'Flanigan. 'Don't try and shemozzle me, you old tripester!' People come over from market to see what is matter. They see two goats lying on grass and me and Clonky and Clinky running around them, chasing O'Flanigan, trying to kick him up his **BABUNSKA**. Soon a big crowd is there.

'Wait!' shouts O'Flanigan, as we chase him round the bend. 'Let me explain.' He kneels by goats and whistles, *Peep! Peep! Up they jump!* Then they starts chasing him too and soon everyone is running all over the shops. The crowd starts clapping and cheerzing. When chasing is over, O'Flanigan explains that goats come from Ireland, his country. They work in quarry, dragging carts full of rock. That's why they grow up so big and strong. To break the rock the men use exploding sticks. **Boom! Boom!** When goats hear big noise, they jump on ground, dead still, and wait for a whistle.

So I am looking at peoples in market. All this chasing and pertoofling around is making them smile, and they doesn't look so sad . . . Slowly I is getting the big idea for a new show. We put up tent in market and gets to work. We tell everybody in town: there is no ticket, you just come. Soon tent is filled to the top.

This is show we give them. Tent is full of dark, music is creeperish. Then a light

is shining out onto Zoltan, a beautiful
snowy-white goaty, stuffing face with
a curly cabbage. 'Ah!' say crowd. But
then Clonky creeps out of shadows,
hiding under hood. He has big gun! We
call it a blonkipump. (Don't be scary—
is not really shooty, just for show.)

BANG!

When crowd sees this, they is doing
booing; guns is reminding them of
war. Too late! *BANG!* Zoltan fall
down! Clonky hops onto Peypa and is

riding around the ring waving his gun, cheerzing, and doing some showings off.

The crowd is boozing like crazy. They doesn't like this show—it is full of badness. Now Clinky runs out in ring dressed in white suit. He leans down and whistles in Zoltan's ear. Up she jumps! Now we turn on big lights so everything is full of bright. Clinky hops onto her back and they is chasing Clonky and Peypa. The crowd is cheerzing like mad for Clinky and boozing their heads off at Clonky. They is chasing around all over the shops! When Clonky jumps off Peypa and tries to run away, Zoltan is chasing him and—**BADONK!**—butts him right in his **BABUNSKA!** The crowd goes monkey bananas! Then I walks out, grabs the blonkipump, fills it with sweeties, and shoots them into crowd. They is chewing and cheerzing and chattering, full of happy. When everything finished, I stand by tent with bucket—maybe someone put coin in. Soon bucket is full. **SKABOONKY!**

Every night I kick the bucket and shout at the stars: 'Look, Grandpappy, look, Pappy—we make good show!' When

spring comes, we is hitting the road—it's
like old times: grey clouds get packed, the
sun starts peeping; trees are leafing, fish
is wriggling. The show is helping Escorvia
to wake up after nightmare. Peoples is
tired of being sad. When we comes to
town, they laughs till they cries and cries
till they laughs. Soon war is forgetful.

But one night, when it time for the big
chase-up, Peypa isn't running away.
She walk slowly out of ring; the crowd
is boozing like mad—they think it all
part of show. When Peypa get to edge
of tent, she fall down. She have no

breaths. I calls for help. Animal doctor
come. He spend long time with Peypa
but it no good. She is sleeping forever.

WHEN LIFE GIVES YOU PATONKLEBERRIES, MAKE HOT CHOCOLATE

Mr Baboomski pulled a spotted handkerchief out of his coat and dabbed his eyes; Zoltan staggered over and gave him a few slobbery licks across the cheek.

'But what happened—why did Peypa die?' I asked.

'Doctor say her body is strong, problem is her heart. I have terrible feeling deep in my gootle; I know why Peypa die. Every night for Zoltan is cheerzing but, when Peypa comes out, everybody starts boozing. The heart gets heavier each night, full of sad; in the end, it is getting broked.'

He paused and stared into the fire. Then he rummaged in his coat and handed me a couple of faded old photographs. The first was of a man in a feathery top hat; he had the biggest moustache I had ever seen. Until I saw the second picture. It showed an older man (Grandpappy, I guessed)—it looked like a pair of squirrels were clinging to his nose while trying to strangle each other.

Mr Baboomski honked into his hankie then sat staring into the fire, stroking his moustache. 'We don't forget Peypa, she always with us.' He pinched the end of his nose and lifted the moustache clean off his face.

'I can never grow big mousetarch like Grandpappy and Pappy; I only gets pricklish bits. When Peypa die, I take snips from tail and make this.' He held up the swirling nest of speckly, grey hair. 'Now I can always remember the ones that are gone; they are in my heart and right under my nose. After Peypa die we stop. I give Clinky and Clonky their share of coins. They sad but now they make up their own show: Clinky fire Clonky out of cannon into big tree. They very popular in Escorvia. I use rest of coins to buy boat ticket for me and Zoltan. So here we is.'

'That's some story. Sounds like you've had a pretty cool life.'

He shrugged. 'Sometimes hot, sometimes cool, sometimes freezing.' He threw another log on the fire. 'Life is a mix-up; you don't know what you gets: happy or sad, cheerzing or boozing. Like Pappy always say: "When life gives you patonkleberries, make hot chocolate." Important thing is to make the best of what you have and be the best you can be because one day you won't.'

'Won't what?'

'Be.'

As we stared in silence at the flames dancing in the stove, I glanced across at Mr Baboomski. He certainly looked and sounded pretty weird but what he said actually made some sense. Why was I moping around just because I had to spend a couple of months at a new school in a different town? It wasn't the end of the world; it might even be quite fun. Zoltan settled down next to me, her great shaggy head resting on my lap.

'I think you is making a new friend,' said Mr Baboomski, his chaotic teeth spreading into a broad grin. 'Good friends is like happiness: too much is never enough. Zoltan has been by my side for years. Now I must bring her home: she work hard, she travel far, time has come to rest in the peaceful, green fields. That is why we come here, to Ireland.'

There was a moments silence, which I broke rather nervously. 'Er, Mr Baboomski?'

'Ja?'

'You're in Cornwall.'

'Cornwhat?!'

HOW TO MAKE ESCORVIAN HOT CHOCOLATE

(Perfect for cold winter's night or sweaty summer afternoon)

Please be doing this:

◎ Milk your goat. If you don't got a goat, cow is OK. (Cat isn't.)

◎ Find a pan (I usually keeps one in coat).

◎ Use fire to roast the milk.

◎ Stir with spoon (also in coat).

◎ Stare at milk until it gets all bubblish.

◎ Keep stirring, keep staring.

◎ Throw in some herbies—anything you can find growing on bush that isn't poisonish is best.

◎ Take favourite choc bar (TWIGS is good but can be sticky) and drown it in milk.

49

- To test, dip in finger. Now dip in toe (can't be too careful). (Remember to wash finger and toe after—never before.)
- Is it too hot or too cold? If both, is ready.
- Serve in a hurry (or mug).
- Get stuffed!

LOVELY SCUBBLY

By the time I had left the trailer and headed back across the fields, the storm had passed and a watery sun was peering through the clouds. The world had looked very different an hour earlier when I'd dashed through the mud and rain, fearful of what awaited me in the trailer.

As it turned out Mr Baboomski was not only friendly but interesting, in a different sort of way. 'Be popping by again if you likes,'

he called as I left. Maybe I would—after all I didn't have any other friends in Trefuggle Bay.

It was still too early for school so I made my way over to the fish factory to see how Dad was getting on. He was standing on the quayside, clutching a clipboard, watching a huge boat docking alongside a massive glass tank. He looked surprised to see me. And worried.

'Did I leave the grill on? Is the cottage on fire?'

'No, Dad, I just got up a bit early to, er—' *have breakfast with a fish-wielding fruitloop who turned out to be a perfectly harmless old circus boss with a detachable moustache and collapsible goat* '—do some homework.'

'Homework already, eh? It's the same at this place,' he grumbled, squinting at his clipboard. 'It never stops!'

'So what's happening?'

He pointed at the boat. 'Well, this is the main business of the day—it's the scubbly trawler, although it doesn't really trawl; actually, it sucks.'

'Looks all right,' I said.

'I mean it uses a high-powered suction pump to catch the fish. Turns out this whole town is built on scubbly. Apparently they only come to spawn in this bay so it's a real local delicacy. People come from miles around to taste it—these fish are like gold bars.'

'LOVELY SCUBBLY!'

The words boomed out across the bay, a dark shadow fell across the tank. I looked up and saw the giant inflatable fish from the Golden Scubbly gliding past. Leaning out of the basket below, bellowing through a megaphone, was an overweight man with a large, bald head. His skin was an oily yellow, like batter; his glassy eyes bulged like pickled onions; his mouth, with its fleshy, ketchup-red lips, gaped open like a fish out of water.

'BREAKFAST SPECIAL TODAY—EXTRA DOLLOP OF MUSHY PEAS WITH EVERY ORDER OVER £50!'

'That's Mayor Pudyn,' explained Dad. He pointed towards the restaurant at the edge of the bay where a long queue was already forming. 'He makes a fortune from the Golden Scubbly. As for this place—' Dad nodded at the damp-looking concrete block looming on the quayside '—the factory owner, Mr Smerkinton-Peck, is cashing in big time.'

So Piers and Hubert's dads were the big cheeses in this fishy town—no wonder the boys thought they ruled the school. With a noisy whine the crane on the back of the boat lowered a floppy rubber tube over the side of the tank. Suddenly, with a tremendous gushing and splashing, the scubbly came pouring out, sending the gulls overhead into a screeching frenzy. I gazed through the glass, hypnotized by the silvery daggers, darting and diving as one. I had never seen anything so beautiful. Somehow it didn't seem right—these amazing-looking creatures were supposed to be rare but they were being hoovered up like there was no tomorrow.

The inside of the factory was even less appealing than the outside. It was a gloomy, joyless place, as grey and miserable as the inside of a week-old fish finger. I followed Dad up some stairs to a cupboard-sized office haunted by the smell of stale fish. There was a panel on the wall with two buttons marked 'In' and

'Out'. The 'In' button was flashing. When Dad pushed it, there was a smooth, gurgling sound as the scubbly entered the factory, shooting in through a glass pipe, like a mercury bullet.

'Half go to the Golden Scubbly; the rest head for the filleting machines and end up in cans.'

'What's this?' I asked, pointing towards the flashing 'Out' button.

'Push it,' said Dad.

A deep rumbling shook the desk and wobbled the filing cabinet, followed by a sludgy, sloppy sound. Finally a gruesome stench rose up through the floorboards. Imagine the stink of a bath of pilchards left out in the sun for a week. Double it. Treble that. You're still not even close. It reeked; honked like a horn; stank for England.

'That's the return journey,' said Dad. 'The filleting waste goes out through a long pipe which runs around the side of the beach and is dumped at sea. That's why there are always seagulls swarming around that edge of the bay. The locals call it Stinker's Cove.'

He pinched his nose and settled down to a mountain of paperwork. 'Better get on with it,' he sighed, sounding like a depressed dalek.

Suddenly the door flew open, flattening me behind it.

'Watkins! I hear your brat of a son has already been causing mayhem at Saint Scubbly's. It won't do. As head of the school governors, I insist on high standards.'

Peering through the crack in the door I could see a tall, thin man in a smart grey suit. He had a razor-sharp nose and mean, beady eyes, just like the eyes of the football-sized seagulls that swooped over the town. Next to him, wearing a gold chain with links shaped like plump little fish, stood Mayor Pudyn, his pickled-onion eyes boggling, his mouth gaping.

Listening to Dad's murmured responses from behind the door—'Yes, Mr Smerkinton-Peck . . . of course, Mr Smerkinton-Peck . . . won't happen again . . .'—I realized why he had spent the previous evening listening to Throaty's album *Workhouse Blues* late into the night. I virtually knew the words to 'I Blew My Boss the Sweetest Raspberry' off by heart.

I gave my boss the good news as I left the production line,

Stick your stinking job where th
     sun will never shine.'
His eyes turned black with fury,
   'Get back and do your duty!'
He pulled his gun, I shot out my
   tongue and nailed him with
   a beauty.

'I'm watching you.' Smerkinton-Peck jabbed a bony finger at Dad. 'And who told you to sit down? Workers stand in my presence—it's the rule!'

They left, slamming the door. Dad raised his eyebrows at me. I explained about the banger and the fight. 'They started it.'

Dad groaned. 'I don't care. As if I didn't have enough to worry about . . . try and stay out of trouble, Tom. If I lose this job, we're sunk.'

When I got to school, Mrs Pudyn was even less interested in hearing my side of the story. I was 'disssss-graccceful', I was 'desssspicable'. I was drenched.

My punishment was to help out in the kitchens every lunchtime for a week. When the bell rang, I wandered over to the kitchen block where, hidden behind a mountain of potatoes, I found the school cook. Mrs Brown was a large, cheerful lady with an explosion of curly ginger hair and bright, sea-green eyes magnified by the thickest glasses I had ever seen. As we peeled the spuds, she gave me the quick version of her life story:

Born and raised in Trefuggle Bay she had married a fisherman. One night, many years ago, there was a terrible storm and Mr Brown didn't arrive for breakfast. The coastguards and other local fishermen searched for days but found nothing. For months afterwards Mrs Brown spent long hours up at Spyglass Point scanning the horizon, hoping to spot the missing boat. All that staring out across the sparkling water had taken its toll on her eyesight. And they never found Mr Brown.

Mrs Brown dashed around the kitchen, squinting into various pots bubbling on the stove, swinging a ladle faster than a Jedi Knight swishing a light-sabre. **SPLOSH!**

A smear of cheese sauce, **GLOOP!**

Now a squirt of custard. That explained why

the fish pie tasted so sweet (not to mention the cheesy tang in the trifle).

Even though it was supposed to be a punishment, working with Mrs Brown was good fun—until it was time to serve lunch. Kitchen hygiene rules meant that I had to wear a scrunchy hairnet thing, which was bright pink. With a frilly chin strap. To keep my uniform clean Mrs Brown lent me her spare apron: the one with 'Please kiss the cook!!!' on the front. As the children drifted in from the playground, I could feel my face turning the same colour as my new hat. Piers and Hubert barged to the front of the queue.

'Sorry, Watkins,' crowed Piers in a loud voice, 'although you do look lovely in that hat, you won't be getting a kiss off me!'

'Huh, huh,' Hubert joined in eventually. 'You got a funny hat on.'

I ignored them and dolloped a portion of pie onto Piers's plate. He didn't move.

'That's a bit mean. Come on, give us some more.'

When I held out the serving spoon again, Piers dragged his plate backwards so that I had to lean right over the counter. Hubert lunged forward, grabbing the chin strap on my hairnet and yanking my head down into the fish pie dish.

SPLUDGE!

'Huh, huh—splatted you.'

Through a steaming mask of mashy, cheesy, custardy scubbly I watched Piers and Hubert roaring with laughter, pointing in my direction, daring the other kids in the queue not to join in the fun.

'What do you look like?' sneered Piers.

Mrs Brown was standing right beside me. She hadn't seen a thing.

They swaggered off, Piers smirking triumphantly, Hubert stooping to lick the mountain of mash he had served himself. I watched them go, anger boiling in my soul, mash cooling on my forehead, and made a silent vow that one day, in the not too distant future, I would take my revenge.

WHEN YOU IS YOUNG, LIFE IS FULL OF CONFUSINGS...

'Boy! **SKABOONKY**! Hungry?'

'I could eat a horse.'

'Do not, hooves is too chewy. Here, get stuffed.'

I accepted the steaming bowl and tucked in greedily. Soon my taste buds were tingling: Mr Baboomski really was an amazing cook. I hadn't expected to return to the old trailer in the corner of the field quite so soon but once I got home from school, heard Throaty yodelling with despair, and saw Dad's glum expression I decided to pop out for some air. I finished the food and leaned back against Zoltan with a burp and a sigh.

Mr Baboomski looked at me keenly, his cross eyes darting this way and that. 'You looks a bit grumplish, boy. What's the prob?'

I told him about my day at school and the

fish pie incident. He listened in silence, twirling the ends of his moustache.

'So these two tripesters is pronking around like mister big bongos—they think they is the juiciest pickles in the cake, eh?'

'Er, yeah, something like that.'

'Hmm. Let me think.' He reached inside his coat and pulled out a slender wooden flute. Soon the trailer was filled with an achingly beautiful, deeply sorrowful melody laced with yearning and desire, heartbreak and pain. A lump rose in my throat; goosebumps covered my skin.

'That was wonderful,' I whispered when he had finished. 'What's it called?'

' "Binkerty Bonkerty Boogie Boogie Bonk"! I maked it up last night when I was sleeping. Music helps me think—my brains is always working betterer when I is making a cheeky racket. So this is what I is thinking: when you is young, life is full of confusings; everybody is hopping about and jiggling around trying to find their place. Sometimes peoples gets treaded on. You see?'

I nodded slowly.

'And if someone is doing too much treading, sometimes you have to say, "Excusing me, please be watching your step or I might have to kick you up the **BABUNSKA**."'

HEY, KID, WE CAN
SEE YOUR WIMPLY!

Escorvia's greatest ever circus show is always finishing with a big parade. Grandpappy and Pappy is leading the way, with pride in their hearts and feathers in their hats. The Spludgy Brothers is coming next, eating swords while juggling live weasels; then Princess Sylvie Starlight, queen of the angry bats, is swinging and swonging through the air; next Jonny Conkez comes jiggling along, singing smoochy songs while escaping from a suit made of chains; after him is Nipsy the monkey, glugging a mug of beer before riding a wild pony through some flaming hoops. All the kids in the circus gets to join in, we is running all over the shops, skipping and tripping, hiding from the clowns (their job is to give us a nice big kick up the **BABUNSKA**—what can be better?).

The final act is Igor the strongman, who is riding around the ring on a unicycle, holding a big cow above his head. The crowd is going crazlepops.

Igor has a son, Petrov—he says he is getting feeded up with being chased by clowns; he wants better part in show. So next time when Igor comes out and is lifting up cow, Petrov follows and picks up a piglet called Minki. The crowds say, 'Eh, look at small boy, he strong, he can lift up piggy!'

Petrov is now the big star and gets bigger than boots. He is ordering other kids around like he is boss. He say, 'People is laughing at your stupido clownish things but when I comes out, everybody is cheerzing.'

I am thinking that his head is getting so big he is floating away, now is time to pop it and bring him back down to ground.

Petrov dresses like his Pappy: bare chest and big, baggy pantaloons. One night before show, I loosen string on Petrov's pantaloons. He walks out in front of crowd, they clap, he bend down to pick up Minki, they cheerz, he lifts

Minki up over his head, they are roaring like nutcrackers. Then, very slowly, his pantaloons are sinking. The crowd is hushed up. Then man shouts, 'Hey, kid, we can see your wimply!'

Soon everybody is crazing with laughter. Petrov drops Minki and tries to run away but his feets are pedalling in the pantaloons. He fall down flat on face with his bare **BABUNSKA** up in air. The crowd is crying, this is funniest show they ever saw.

After that, Petrov is not so noisy.

GOAT RIDER

'It must have been so cool growing up in the circus—at least you didn't have to sit in boring lessons at some stupid, fishy old school.'

Mr Baboomski shrugged. 'You can be finding learnings all over the place.' He reached inside his coat and pulled out some onions which he started to juggle. He tossed them in my direction. 'Here, boy, try your luck.'

And so began my lessons in circus skills: I started with juggling, moved on to level-one clowning and, in no time, was having a go at fire-eating for beginners. Mr Baboomski was a brilliant teacher, far better than anyone at Saint Scubbly's. I had been feeling pretty down about life in Cornwall—I still longed for Mum's Special Project to end so everything could get back to normal—but the sense of achievement I got from learning all this new stuff really boosted my confidence. As a way of saying thank you, I decided to set myself a

Special Project: I would help him get Zoltan back to Ireland. But how?

The problem was simple: cash. Mr Baboomski had blown all his savings on the first ferry ticket; now he needed to earn some more to buy another.

'Why don't you put on a show here?' I suggested, keeping a close eye on the oranges I was juggling. 'I'm sure people would come.'

'My circus days is all in my behind now.' He stroked his moustache and sighed. 'That last show with Peypa . . . it is the end for me. Now I just wants to give Zoltan a quiet life.'

'In that case, we need to find you some other kind of work.'

And that was where it got complicated. Even if he removed the crooked top hat (and even more crooked moustache) that still left the straggly hair, wandering eyes, snaggly teeth, and tendency to shout '**SKABOONKY**!' I didn't fancy his chances in a job interview.

Then I had an idea. I knew someone who needed help and wouldn't focus too closely on his appearance—with her eyesight she struggled to focus on anything. I made the necessary introductions after school one day and left them to it. They got on like a kitchen on fire.

'He's quite a character, your Mr Bambyboomyski,' Mrs Brown chuckled. 'The stories he tells . . . and he knows his way around a frying pan, and as for the ingredients he brings me . . . See that?' she said proudly, waving a purple, mud-caked knobbly thing. 'That's a scootlepop!'

Mr Baboomski sounded just as happy. 'This Mrs Brown makes **SKABOONKY** cookings. She nearly as blind as old Mister Klunkenpop, Escorvia's champion knife-thrower. I never forget the way the crowds scream for his act—especially in front row. And she is learning me some proper best English—"Good mornings, how did you do?" "We are having some weather today—it is raining like a cat and a dog, but mustn't crumble." '

I, on the other hand, was finding it harder to make new friends. After the banger and fish pie incidents, the other kids kept their distance, knowing that Piers and Hubert would target anyone seen talking to me. Rather than mope around the playground on my own, I started sneaking off after lunch for walks

along the cliffs
with Zoltan. I
told her everything:
about missing Mum,
Dad's gloominess, the
problems at school.
This might sound weird
but Zoltan was a really
great listener—head
cocked on one side, gazing
at me steadily. If I was a bit down, she
would lean her head on my shoulder, catching
me under the chin with a slobbery lick or two.
We usually ended up on top of Spyglass Point,
gazing out to sea. At that point in my life it
was probably my favourite place in the whole
world and, I guess, Zoltan was my best friend.
Somehow it felt like we were both stuck in
the wrong place, wondering how to get home.

The day after school broke up for the summer
holidays, I headed up the cliff path on a bright,
cloudless morning.

'Eh! Boy! You just in time. Chase me.'

We walked around the foot of Spyglass Point

and carried on across the fields. Every so often Mr Baboomski would yank a tuft of greenery out of the ground or scoop a handful of berries from a hedge. By the time we arrived at the edge of the cliffs, his hat was full to the brim.

'We go down,' said Mr Baboomski.

'You're crazy!' I said. 'We'll break our necks.'

He raised his palms. 'Don't be scary, boy.'

I watched Zoltan step cautiously down onto the rocks and disappear from view. Great, I thought, she's fallen into the sea—and this time she really is dead. But then a pink nose popped up between the rocks and I saw those familiar dreamy eyes gazing at me.

'Pieces of cakes,' said Mr Baboomski cheerfully. 'Just watch where she put her foots and puts your foots in same place.'

I lowered myself gingerly onto a sandy shelf just under the clifftop; far below the sea boiled and foamed. Following Zoltan's lead I clambered and slithered over the rocks as we descended slowly down the cliff. Mr Baboomski came down last. Soon we reached an ancient flight of grey stone steps which led down to a tiny beach nestled beneath the overhanging cliff face. Above us the cold, grey stone wall of the fish factory loomed behind the jagged rocks. Mr Baboomski ruffled my hair.

'You see, boy,' he grinned, eyes rolling in all directions, 'we not crazy—we out to lunch!'

From his coat he produced a stick with a line dangling from one end, then tiptoed along a narrow ledge of rock behind the factory and crouched next to a tidal pool. In no time he was back with a healthy-sized scubbly and an armful of sticks. More rummaging in the coat produced a frying pan, some matches, and a picnic blanket. The fish, garnished with a hatful of greens and berries, was lip-smackingly delicious. When we had finished, he produced a small paper bag; peering inside I saw half a dozen lilac-coloured balls.

'Special Escorvian treats,' explained Mr Baboomski. 'We calls them koppletops.' He handed me a stick. 'Here—make it sticky.'

I skewered one of the little balls and held it over the glowing embers. It turned pink, then orange, then started to crackle and burn.

'Eat it flaming quick!' yelled Mr Baboomski.

When my teeth cracked the baked outer shell of the koppletop, spicy, sugary splinters fizzed on my tongue which instantly dissolved into a syrupy honey oozing down my throat. It tasted so weirdly amazing, I burst out laughing.

'What's in it?' I giggled stickily.

Mr Baboomski tapped the side of his nose.

'Grandpappy tell Pappy, Pappy tell me. This is how we finish each day in circus, sitting by fire eating koppletops. Sometimes we is telling stories—Madame Zootzer always makes me scary, I still have nightie mares thinking about the cheesy ghost and the midnight chicken!' He shuddered, lifted another crackling ball out of the fire, and then, with a flick of his wrist, sent it flying into the air. 'Ayoop!'

Zoltan leaned her neck back lazily and let the koppletop fall into her gaping mouth. She stood there quietly slurping, her eyes even more dreamy than usual.

Mr Baboomski got up, stretched, then gathered up the picnic blanket.

'Now, boy, I teach you extra special trick.'

He held the blanket out straight in front of him and waggled it in Zoltan's direction. She gazed at him casually for a few seconds, gave a little sniff, lowered her head, and charged. I'd only ever seen Zoltan ambling about the place before and now suddenly she was belting up the beach like a speeding bullet. A split second before she reached him Mr Baboomski spun around, whipped away the blanket, and let the turbo-charged goat zoom by.

He grinned toothily. 'Now you tries.'

I held up my hands in protest. 'You're joking—I couldn't do that.'

'No jokings. Come, I show you.'

It's not easy standing still watching a pair of pointy horns torpedoing towards you. Several times I ended up face down in the sand having dived for cover at the last moment. But with some gentle guidance from Mr Baboomski it wasn't too long before I was swerving and swaying pretty well.

'Is good,' said Mr Baboomski, 'but now for the trick that made Nipsy Escorvia's superstar chimp.

Next time Zoltan is coming, grab a horn and hop sideways. **UPADOOF**! You is riding goat!'

'What? I'll never manage that!' I protested.

'Be trying, see what can happen.'

I took up my position again. As Zoltan rushed forwards, my heart began to pound—this was never going to work. As she sped past me, I dropped the blanket, grabbed a horn, and shut my eyes. When I opened them, I expected to be face down in the sand, a trail of hoof prints across my back. But I wasn't, I was flying! Racing up the beach on Zoltan's back, the wind whipping into my face.

'SKABOONKY!'

I yelled and punched the air with my fists. That was when I ended up face down in the sand.

Mr Baboomski helped me up; Zoltan trotted over and gave me drooly lick on the cheek.

'You can do it —I told you,' he grinned. 'We can practise riding with no hands another day.'

The sun was sinking towards the horizon as we made our way back up the cliffs. Mr Baboomski went up first and was soon out of sight.

'I'm stuck,' I said to no one in particular when I reached the top of the steps.

Then I felt a gentle nudge in the ribs. Zoltan flicked her head back, pushing me behind her. I climbed carefully onto her back and put my arms gently around her neck. She tottered forwards, then, with a powerful kick of her hind legs, hopped onto a flat rock. The sight of the sea pounding the jagged rocks far below made my scubbly rise—I shut my eyes and buried my face in Zoltan's shaggy fur, breathing in her warm goaty smell. She was so sure-footed that soon I had forgotten my fear and was tossing back my head and laughing as she sprang and skipped effortlessly up the steep, craggy cliff. All too soon we were back in the field in front of a laughing Mr Baboomski.

'Hey, boy—you rides goat better than a drunken monkey!'

There are certain phrases a boy of my age might want to hear: 'Well done, Watkins, you've got an A+' or maybe 'Congratulations, Tom, I'm making you captain of the football team.' 'Hey, boy—you rides goat better than a drunken monkey!' was a bit unusual but it did the trick. A lump the size of a koppletop rose in

my throat; the low sun made my eyes prickle. I hugged Mr Baboomski a bit sheepishly and Zoltan (a bit goatishly) and wandered back across the fields.

It had been a perfect day and it was about to get even better. Back at the cottage there was loud music blaring but for once it wasn't Throaty—it was some kind of jazzy, trumpetish business that provided the perfect soundtrack to Dad's crazy skittering about. For the first time in ages he looked really excited.

'Your mother, coming back for a couple of weeks, arriving tomorrow,' he said breathlessly. 'Here.' He thrust a bucket full of cleaning stuff at me. 'I'll carry on in here, you go and attack the bathroom.'

That night I reckon I became the first person in history to shed a tear of happiness while plunging a blocked toilet.

HOW TO MAKE
KOPPLETOPS

- Be choosing a nice, bright sunny day (like Wednesday).
- Start a fire in a safe place (like beach or bath or hat).
- Choose your favourite pan (I calls mine Peter, sometimes Dave for shorts).
- Gather some herbies (anything not poisonish) and chop them until they is feeling fine.
- Squeeze the life out of a fresh pignut.
- Add the zest of a nest.
- Whisk until it is whisky.
- Prepare a bed of rice (you might want some snorings later, cookings is tirish).
- Now strain (if you is going purplish, you is straining too much).

- Dice a pickled pogglesnip. Now roll the dice. Six! You gets the first koppletop!
- Grate something great into the mix.
- Let it simmer for a few minutes. If it is still looking a bit grumplish, give it another few minutes.
- Sprinkle on some sprinkles.
- Lean over pan and ask clown to tell joke, like: Knocking, knocking!—Who is being there?—Pomple—Pomple who?—Pomple badomples, that's who!
- Add secret ingredient.
- Serve by the fireside with friends and a story from Madame Zootzer (not the one about the mouse who winked—that makes me patoof myself).
- GET STUFFED!

FLUTUADOR FLIGHTS
AND FIGHTS

Early that morning I heard a taxi pulling up outside the cottage and nearly fell downstairs in my rush to get to the door. An elegant, tanned lady in a white business suit stood there. Mum? I couldn't believe my eyes: it was like one of those TV shows where they take an ordinary person off the street and give them a proper going over. Dad drifted downstairs—rumpled and sleepy in his striped pyjamas, rubbing his stubbly chin, bed-head hair standing up like a shark fin—and gawped at the visitor. He looked like a character from a science-fiction film who is summoned through time and space in the middle of the night to meet a superior alien life form.

Things were a bit awkward at first. Dad clattered around the kitchen making a huge fry-up, but his ears pricked up when Mum mentioned some of the rock stars that were hanging out at Dr Smoothy's place on Questimu.

'You met Jasper "Twelve Fingers" O'Toole? Only the greatest keyboardist since . . . What? Jimmy "the Jiggler" Maracas? Man, that cat could shake. He did that cool debut album . . .'

'Smoking like crazy!' shouted Mum.

'No, I think that was his second album.'

'Flaming curtains!' I yelled.

'Don't be daft, Tom,' snorted Dad. '*Flaming Curtains* was by Jonny and the Widgets.'

Once we had put out the kitchen fire, binned the charred fry-up, and had some Weetabites, Mum opened her suitcase and pulled out a cardboard box.

'I got you a present, Tom.'

Inside the box was a lemon-shaped piece of wood, about the size of my head; it felt as light as a feather. 'It's a flutuador,' Mum explained. 'All the kids in Questimu have them. Come on, I'll show you how it works.'

Despite the bright sunshine the beach was deserted.

'OK, Tom, now throw it as high as you can into the air.'

'But what if I don't catch it?'

'It'll be fine—trust me.'

I flung the flutuador into the blue sky. As it started to drop, I raced after it. Suddenly it changed shape from smooth and rounded to sharp and spikey, like a giant fir cone. Then it began to spin slowly, drifting across the beach. When it finally came back down, it landed gently in my arms. Mum pointed to the criss-cross shapes on its surface.

'These are tiny flaps that catch in the breeze; in the warm currents around Questimu, flutuadors can float forever.'

As we walked along the beach chatting and chasing after the flutuador, Mum asked, 'How's school—made any nice, new friends?'

I wanted to tell her everything about Zoltan and Mr Baboomski and my own Special Project to help my new friends get back to Ireland, but I didn't. Mum would probably freak at the thought of me hanging around with a slightly shabby Escorvian circus boss and his trusty stunt goat so I just nodded vaguely, muttered, 'It's all fine,' and gave the flutuador another massive heave into the air.

I wanted the holidays to last forever but all too soon Mum flew back to her Special Project, Dad was back to work, and grumpiness and I was off to school. Our term project was on 'International Cultures' so I chose Questimu and even brought in the flutuador when it was my turn to give a talk.

When I had finished, Miss Thompson tweaked the edge of her glasses a few times then said, 'I wonder if perhaps, Watkins, you might give us a demonstration?' A murmur of approval swept around the classroom. Piers yawned like a hippo.

Once everyone had gathered at the top of the playground, I threw the flutuador as high as I could into the air. It zigzagged across the playground, followed by a cheering mob. For once everyone seemed to be having fun— 'That's so cool!' 'Me next, Tom!' 'Let's have a go, Watkins!' Having felt invisible for months, suddenly I was the centre of attention. Of course, not everyone was joining in. Piers leaned against the wall at the far end of the playground, headphones on, eyes glued on his New Wave Deluxe Gamestation. Eventually even Hubert left his side and puffed away at the back of the chasing pack. When he finally caught the flutuador, something amazing happened— Hubert actually smiled. Piers pushed himself away from the wall and slunk over. He lifted the flutuador out of Hubert's arms and examined it. 'Wow. What a fascinating bit of wood,' he said sarcastically. 'Can I have a go?'

He crouched down and flung the flutuador two-handed into the air. But, rather than aim in the direction of the playground, he threw it backwards—over the school wall.

'Oops, silly me,' he said with a nasty smirk.

The flutuador caught a stiff sea breeze and floated away, eventually landing in the middle of the main road, in the path of a truck rumbling up from the fish factory. Ignoring Miss Thompson's panicky cries, I ran out of the school gates, shouting and waving my arms, trying to catch the driver's attention, but to no avail. The truck sped past, crushing the flutuador under its tyres. I nipped into the road, gathered up a couple of the larger pieces, then stomped back towards the school.

Miss Thompson took one look at my face and began fiddling madly with her glasses. 'Now, Piers, I think you really ought to apologize to Watkins. That was rather clumsy.'

'I'm so sorry,' said Piers sarcastically before replacing his headphones and turning his back. I didn't think twice.

THWACK!

A backhand swipe sent the headphones flying across the playground. Piers spun around, his piggy little eyes blazing with fury. He nodded towards his bodyguard who advanced towards me, fists clenched, baring teeth glued together with double-fudge nougat.

I looked around. Where was my back-up? Who was on my side? A few minutes earlier the other kids had been all over me; now they shrank back. Miss Thompson was yanking at her fringe, trying to disappear behind a curtain of hair. I had the familiar sensation of being completely alone. Then, out of the corner of my eye, I spotted a figure heading towards us from the direction of the kitchen block and felt a warm surge of relief.

The cavalry was on its way.

A NICE BIG KICK UP THE BABUNSKA

Mr Baboomski ambled across the playground, whistling and waving. I grinned and was about to wave back when I spotted the expressions on my classmates' faces. I looked back at the figure loping towards us and saw what they saw: tangled curtains of hair tumbling from a crumpled top hat; crazily darting eyes; a shaggy moustache so littered with food it read like a lunch menu; a filthy, moth-eaten coat. He marched up to me and beamed, baring his gappy, snaggly teeth.

'Boy! **SKABOONKY**!'

'Ska—what?' sneered Piers, a look of utter disgust creasing his sharp features. 'Watkins, do you actually know this . . . person?'

I glanced around at the expectant faces ogling me from all directions and panicked.

'No,' I muttered. Mr Baboomski's cheerful grin slipped into a frown of confusion.

'What? Speak up!' snapped Piers.

'No,' I said a little louder, staring at my shoes, 'I've never seen him before.'

When I finally looked up, Mr Baboomski was gazing at me curiously; for once his eyes were completely still.

'Sorry,' he said hoarsely. 'I have mistook you for somebody else.'

He shuffled off accompanied by a chorus of snorts and sniggers from Piers and Hubert.

'Are you sure he's not a chum of yours, Watkins?' chuckled Piers, pinching the tip of his pointy nose. 'Only, he was also a bit whiffy!'

The tiny cottage we were staying in was downwind of the factory. As a result, even when it had been washed and hung on the line, my school uniform always gave off a slightly fishy pong, something Piers never missed a chance to point out.

I was studying my feet again, occasionally glancing up at the hunched figure shambling off into the distance. Like a hungry shark, Piers smelt blood.

'It's your choice, Watkins, but I should warn you, not everyone likes hanging around with stinkers. I expect that's why your mum had to escape to the other side of the world—she probably couldn't wait to get away.'

A boiling wave of anger washed over me. Blinded by rage, images flashed before my eyes: me and Mum on the beach playing with the flutuador; Piers' smirk as he threw it over the wall; the look on Mr Baboomski's face as he slunk away . . .

Piers bent down to pick up his headphones. Suddenly the pictures in my mind melted away until all I could see was a pair of sleepy eyes the colour of liquid honey gazing at me, waiting for my next move. Somewhere, deep in the back of my brain, I heard a familiar voice: 'A nice big kick up the **BABUNSKA**—what can be better?'

90

I caught Piers with a beauty. In fact, I probably gave it too much welly—when he went sprawling onto the playground, I landed on top of him. His wails for help were quickly answered. Hubert bundled in and soon we were just a blur of arms and legs thrashing around like a drunken octopus while Miss Thompson shrieked helplessly. With Hubert lying on me like a beached whale, I was pretty helpless too but when he scrambled to his feet, I just managed to grab his leg. As he struggled to shake me off, roaring with anger, his trousers slid slowly south revealing a pair of midnight blue Y-fronts covered in silver stars. He staggered forward, trousers twisted around his ankles, and wobbled for a few seconds then—**THUMP!**—fell backwards on top of me, his backside using my face as a landing pad. Suddenly I was seeing stars . . . and a half moon.

That really knocked the wind out of me. Sadly it did the same for Hubert. A noise like a brass band chasing a herd of terrified geese through a tunnel echoed around the playground:

PARPERTY-PARP! HONK! HONK! QUACK! QUACK!

When I finally got to my feet, a sea of faces swirled before me: Miss Thompson, white as snow, hands clasped over her mouth; Piers, roaring with laughter, pointing at me; Hubert, grinning idiotically; the other children, holding their noses, caught halfway between horror and laughter; Mrs Pudyn, glaring through her office window, mouthing furiously, spraying a monsoon of spit onto the glass.

I ran.

Through the school gates, down the high street, up the hill, across the fields, and along the cliffs—I didn't stop until I reached the top of Spyglass Point. I gazed out to sea, panting. Now what? I certainly couldn't face going back to school. Normally I would have headed down to the battered old trailer but I didn't dare do that either. Mr Baboomski must hate me. After all his kindness and friendship I had been too embarrassed to admit that I even knew him. Why? Just because I was worried what Piers and a few other kids I barely knew might say. I don't think I have ever felt so ashamed in my life. Or, for that matter, so alone.

Then I felt a warm nose nuzzling the back of my hand.

'Zoltan! Where did you spring from? What are you, some kind of ninja goat?'

She lowered a sleepy eyelid. I was so happy to see her I could have cried. A few minutes later, when I told her about the scene in the playground, the tears did come. Then we sat in silence for what seemed like hours, watching the sun sink slowly towards the sea.

NEVER FORGET
TO REMEMBER
WHO YOU IS

Is difficult when you is growing—lots of confusings about who is what and where is you.

When I am starting in circus, I is always doings the worst jobs: cleaning up pootle from the animals; getting sawed in half by the Great Gazonkski; helping Clinky and Clonky practise their **BABUNSKA**-kicking; standing very still and sweaty while old Mister Klunkenpop does his knife-throwings; trying to give the Spludgy Brothers' ferrets their monthly bath. Sometimes I is getting feeded up with circus life.

One day we is taking circus to big city. I go for walk and find some big boys hanging around. They has fancy clothes and combed hair and is doing chewing with gum. I think I wants to be like them. Then Pappy comes along with shovel. 'Come,' he say to me. 'Is nearly time for show and there is horsie droplings all around.'

Biggest boy is sniggling. He say to Pappy, 'Hey, mister, I likes your whiskers—is you one of the clowns?' The other boys laugh. I looks at Pappy, then I looks at boys. Then I laughs too.

Pappy walks up to biggest boy. 'Yes,' he say, 'I is clown. Let me tell you joke: what starts with b and is stinging a lot.'

Big boy is snerkling. 'Easy,' he say.
'A bee.'

Pappy smile. 'Wrong, is
BABUNSKA.' WHOOSH!
CLANG! He swings shovel and catches
boy—SPLAT!—on his seat. Boy howls
louder than the hairy ghost in Madame
Zootzer's story about the midnight
chicken!

WHOOSH!
CLANG!
WHOOSH! CLANG!
WHOOSH! CLANG!

Soon all boys is running away
grabbing their stinging cheeks.

Pappy looks at me. My cheeks (the ones

on face) is also stinging, with shames. 'Listen, boy,' he say. 'World is big, full of peoples and places, but promise me this: never forget to remember who you is.' He smiles and skuffles my hairs. Then he hand me shovel.

'Now go and clean up the pootle, dinglebrain.' And he give me a softie kick up **BABUNSKA** for good luck.

BLOW YOUR OWN HONKER

At dusk we headed back through the fields. Sitting up at Spyglass Point I had plucked up the courage to at least offer Mr Baboomski an apology—although I wouldn't have blamed him if he told me to 'get packed!'.

The trailer was deserted but a cheery fire flickered in the stove. Suddenly he appeared, tumbling through a hedge backwards, clutching a hatful of goodies.

'Boy! **SKABOONKY**!'

'Um, look, Mr Baboomski,' I began awkwardly, 'I just wanted to say, about earlier, when I pretended not to know you—it was really stupid, I . . .'

He raised his palms to silence me. 'Is no problems. Like Mrs Brown say: there's no points for crying over split milk.

While he served up some delicious scubbly fried in patonkleberries I told him about the fight. 'What really bugged me was Piers talking about Mum. What does he know about it? Nothing, that's what. She's actually doing a very important job over there. As if she's trying to escape. Huh!'

As I stared at the fire, the dancing flames started to make my eyes water. Zoltan trotted over and gave me a couple of slobbery licks under the chin. Mr Baboomski put his arm around my shoulders and fished a spotted hankie from his sleeve.

'Here, boy, blow your own honker.'

When I took the hankie, I saw that another was knotted to the corner. And another. And another! Soon there were dozens of them, streaming like bunting out of Mr Baboomski's sleeve. His hat flew off, his eyes rolled, his moustache began to twirl.

'Eh! Oi! Oi! What happens?' Now they were pouring from his trouser leg.

In no time I was crying with laughter. The old circus boss ruffled my hair and dabbed the corner of his mouth delicately with the snake of brightly coloured cloth spilling all over the trailer.

'Mrs Brown is teaching me best English manners. Now be stuffing your cake-hole please, thank you—is koppletops for pud.'

'These are so brilliant,' I said, rivers of treaclish delight running down my chin. 'You've got to tell me what's in them.'

Mr Baboomski tapped the side of his nose, crossing his eyes mysteriously. 'Nobody knows.'

'But how do you—'

He tapped his nose again, accidentally swiping his moustache into the pan on top of the stove. He yelped, flicking the hairy nest out of the frying pan into the fire and then onto the floor.

'So, boy!' he shouted, jigging around as he stamped on the flaming moustache. 'You feels better now?'

'Much better, thanks.

It just annoys me that two boys can make everyone's life at school so miserable—I just wish there was something I could do to put Piers and Hubert in their place.'

He stopped jigging and looked at me solemnly. 'Boy, when monkey steals your peanuts, it's time for some chimpy soup.'

I nodded. A few moments passed in silence.

'Er, what does that mean, exactly?'

Mr Baboomski jammed his crooked hat onto his head; a few herbs fluttered down into his dangly, chaotic hair. From somewhere deep in his overcoat he dug out his long, thin pipe. It was already smoking. Finally, he clipped on his moustache. It was also smoking.

'It means the time has come to fight back.'

ALWAYS USE YOUR HEAD (ESPECIALLY WHEN THERE IS A MONKEY SNOOZING ON IT)

When Escorvia is warring with itself, circus is keeping on the road—trying to stay out of troubles. The road is hard and dusty: our feets is singing a sad song, our tongues is flopping around like a fish in a hat. One day we spies a beautiful river, sploshing and sparkly. At last we can drink and dip our howling toes.

But, just as we is crossing field towards river, mens jump out from behind trees. They is holding sticks and carrying a teared-up flag; they looks tired, dirty, and grumplish. The leader steps forward.

'You can't walk here,' he say.

I shows him the front of my hands. 'We is just walking to the river, my friend.'

'No, you isn't,' he snerks. 'This is our field now—get packed or I will bonk you on the honker!'

He is full of crossness, scratching for a fight. I smile and pinch the end of my honker. At the same time I is squeezing a little horn in my pocket.

HONK! HONK! HONK!

honks my honker.

The leader is still scowly but some of the mens behind him is getting grinnish.

'Oh, so you're a cheeky monkey,

eh?' he say, wobbling his fist near my chops.

'No, but he is.' I lift my hat and there is Nipsy, curled on my head, snoring like thunders.

Now mens is starting to laugh but still leader is grumplish.

'Be shovelling off,' he growls.

'OK,' I says, 'keep your hairs on.' Then I do a big sneeze so that mousetarch flies up in air. 'Oops—easier said than done!'

Nipsy wakes with a SKOOKARK!, leaps off my nut, grabs mousetarch, and is wearing it like wig.

'Oi! Give it back you tripester! Grab him!' Clonky swings a boot at the cheeky chimp, misses, and catches me perfectly

in the **BABUNSKA**—'Oof!' 1 is
rolling over the field trying to grab the
hairy little thief who is wigging and
wiggling around all over the shops.

Mens is laughing and cheerzing like
crazlepops.

When I finally gets back to feet with mousetarch in place, one of mens say to leader, 'Come on Vlad, let them pass. We are feeded up with fighting but were starving for some laughings.'

The leader walks up close until his breathing is in my face and raises his hand. He pushes my nose. HONK! He smiles and straightens my mousetarch. 'River is that way,' he say.

In life there is many ways to fight for what you needs—the important thing is to always use your head, especially when there is a monkey snoozing on it!

LISTEN TO YOUR HEART, BREATHE WITH YOUR EARS

In a film this would be the part where the exciting music kicks in and you watch me start out really rubbish at something but gradually get better until, in super slow motion, I turn into an absolute world-beater. You know the sort of thing: one minute the young kung fu apprentice can barely hold a pair of chop sticks; the next he's a psycho ninja. Unfortunately real life doesn't work like that, as I quickly discovered when I reported to Mr Baboomski's trailer the following day. I had hoped he would have a brilliant plan up his sleeve (he seemed to have pretty much everything else up there) but he didn't—just a trailer full of old circus stuff.

'This place is like a pig style,' he said proudly, burrowing through piles of clutter.

'What's this?' I reached under his chair and

pulled out a weird-looking object that was part rifle, part brass trumpet.

'That is blonkipump. Remember I told you—in circus we use it to shoot sweeties at kids in crowd.'

'That's perfect! I could load it up with stinkbombs, hide in the bushes near the school gates, and let Piers and Hubert have it!'

Mr Baboomski shook his head sadly. 'Is not right, boy. Circus is about putting on show, making peoples happy, not sneakering around attacking them.'

'But you said it was time to fight back. I thought we were going to put Piers and Hubert in their place.'

'We is,' replied Mr Baboomski, 'but not by shooting some stink at them. There is different ways to fight—sometimes you have to use your head. Here is plan: you is going to show other kids at school some circus tricks. They will say, "Hey, bongo! I likes this, I wants to join in." Soon everybody will be having a good time except those tripesters who will be all left out. That is how you puts them in their place.'

Maybe he had a point. When we were chasing the flutuador around the playground, the other kids had actually been having fun for once. Piers couldn't stand it and had to ruin everything. If I could get everyone involved in doing some fun circus stuff, maybe people would feel more confident about standing up to Piers if he tried to butt in. But was I feeling confident enough to show off my new skills? What if Piers and Hubert wrecked it from the start? What if the other kids laughed at me? Even worse, what if everyone thought circus skills were stupid or boring?

Mr Baboomski seemed to read my mind. 'Don't be worryful, boy. Is not easy doing show—first time I try I nearly patoof myself.'

'But what if people laugh at me?'

Mr Baboomski lifted his top hat, revealing a startled-looking rabbit nibbling a parsnip. 'Let them. Sometimes peoples laugh at you, sometimes they laugh with you, sometimes they laugh under or over you. Once someone laughed right through me—it was quite tickerlish. Sounds like kids in your school might be hungry for some laughings. School is not good place today; you can make it better tomorrow. You can only fail if you don't try.'

'I guess so. But what can I do to really grab their attention?'

He reached under the bed and pulled out some stilts. 'You is already a good juggler—how about doing it up in sky on these wobble sticks?'

I groaned. 'I'll never manage that.'

Mr Baboomski pulled out his pipe and puffed thoughtfully; turquoise bubbles streamed into the air. He frowned.

'Eh? What the—? Listen, boy, I tell you story. Many years ago I wanted to be like the angry bats, zootzing through the air. I used to watch Princess Sylvie Starlight leap off one swing, perform a triple somersault, then catch the other swing in her teeth—CHOMP! Such style! Such elegance! One day, Pappy says he will teach me. I am too scary but he say, "Don't be worryful—you jump, I catch." So we climbs to top of tent and starts swinging and swonging. Only problems: when I looks down I nearly patoof myself. "So don't look, dinglebrain!" shouts Pappy. I shut eyes, takes deep breath, and . . . AYOOP!'

Mr Baboomski grinned gappily, his eyes rolling with delight, and his arms outstretched.

'Now I is flying like a bird, swooping and swonking. It is like dream. Then I feel a hand grip mine. Pappy catch me! I do it! I am king of the world! I cheerzed like a crazy and punched my fist in the air. But I miss air and bonk Pappy on his honker. He say, "Oof! My honker!" and is letting go. Luckily horses are training below and I have soft landing in pile of droplings.'

I stared at him blankly.

'So you see, boy: even when you soar like eagle, you can still land in a pile of pootle. This is life. But it don't stop you trying to fly.'

We stepped out of the trailer and Mr Baboomski leaned the stilts against a tree stump, making a long, narrow ramp.

'Here, boy, first you finds your balance—careful, it might be hiding.'

'Nah, that's easy.' I hopped onto the stilts, took a few steps forward, wobbled like mad, and

fell onto the grass.
After a dozen more
failed attempts I
was getting pretty
cross. Zoltan
ambled over and
strode elegantly
and effortlessly

up and down the stilty ramp. She tossed her head, beckoning me to follow. Now I can't say why but somehow the reassuring sight of that huge goat in front of me did the trick. Soon I was dancing up and down the narrow ramp with ease. Zoltan lowered a sleepy eyelid and wandered off.

'**SKABOONKY**!' yelled Mr Baboomski. 'Now you try standing up.'

I spent the next few hours tottering around like a sea-sick giraffe, never managing more than a few steps before coming crashing down to earth. In no time I was covered in mud and bruises. Falling down was bad enough but what really started to annoy me was Mr Baboomski's shouts of encouragement. They probably made sense in Escorvian but in English . . .

'Walk tall! Kiss the stars, lick the moon!'

'Open your mind, shut your face!'

'The truth is at the bottom of your heart; the power is at the heart of your bottom!'

'I think you're confusing me with Hubert!' I shouted, collapsing backwards into a bed of nettles where a monstrous cowpat broke my fall.

By the time I had finally found my balance, darkness was closing in and a steady drizzle was blowing in off the sea. All I really wanted to do was limp home and fall on my bed. Mr Baboomski produced a handful of grimy potatoes from inside his coat and passed them up to me.

'Don't smell the fear—it stinks!' he whispered. 'Sniff with your mind!'

I steadied myself, took a deep breath, and tossed the spuds into the air . . . and kept them there! I was doing it, I was juggling on stilts!

'SKABOONKY!' yelled Mr Baboomski and clapped me on the back. Except my back was several feet above him so what he actually clapped was one of the stilts.

The potatoes flew one way and I went the other, landing in a patch of gorse with a soft thud. Wedged in the prickly bush, I watched helplessly as the spuds looped in my direction—now we had the slow-mo movie effect. They landed on my head one by one— **DOINK! DOINK! DOINK! DOINK!**

Mr Baboomski wandered over. 'You is getting

there—next time listen to your heart, breathe with your ears.'

Breathe with my what?! I was aching all over, starving, cold, wet, and covered in nettle stings, gorse prickles, and cow dung. Most of all I was angry: with rubbish old Trefuggle Bay, stupid Saint Scubbly's, with Piers and Hubert, with Mum and Dad—with everything and everyone.

'Come on, boy,' said Mr Baboomski cheerfully, 'we try once more today then start again tomorrow—is no time for lazing around in bush.'

Lazing around?! That did it. I scrambled out of the gorse and hurled the stilts to the ground.

'I won't be coming back tomorrow,' I snapped. 'Or the day after—or ever. In fact, I wouldn't care if I never saw you again!'

Far in the distance, over at Stinker's Cove, angry seagulls shrieked and cawed. Without another word, I stomped home.

I spent the evening and most of the next day sulking but by teatime on Sunday I was starting to feel really guilty. After all, Mr Baboomski had only been trying to help. He may have had runaway teeth, cross eyes, and a portable moustache but his heart was definitely in the right place. How could I have said such a terrible thing?

I decided to go and apologize and wandered off up the path towards the cliffs. I pushed open the gate and walked into the field then stopped dead in my tracks. I blinked, rubbed my eyes, even slapped myself around the face to check I wasn't dreaming. But nothing could change the loopy messages my eyes were sending to my brain: Mr Baboomski's trailer had disappeared. But that was only the half of it. Spyglass Point was gone too.

I couldn't believe my eyes—how could a massive chunk of rock just vanish into thin air? Then the sky started wobbling. The patch of blue above the corner of the cliffs where Spyglass Point had stood was shimmying all over the place! I stumbled forward into the field, eyes fixed on the jiggling sky. It was only when I heard a rustling sound that I finally realized what was going on. Spyglass Point hadn't disappeared—it was hidden by a tower of scaffolding wrapped in sky-blue tarpaulin. A barbed wire fence surrounded the tower, on which a sign read:

> **Danger. Building site.**
>
> # KEEP OUT.
> ## (Smerkinton-Peck Enterprises)

But where was Mr Baboomski's trailer? Then I spotted something that made my heart lurch—tyre tracks leading across the fields, heading for the edge of the cliff. I sprinted after them, charging into the gusting wind. My mind raced faster than my feet, churning out questions, juggling hope and despair. Why? How? What if? Maybe? But when I reached the edge of the cliff, the answer I had dreaded most was spread out before me.

Far below, shattered on the rocks, scattered across the beach, lay the remains of Mr Baboomski's trailer. The scene was eerily still, the only movement coming from a crumpled old top hat, drifting and twirling in the gently lapping shallows.

A VERY FISHY BUSINESS

I scrambled down the cliffs, sliding and stumbling, blinded by tears and the biting wind. Down on the beach I started picking through the wreckage, expecting the worst. There was no sign of Mr Baboomski or Zoltan. I rescued his hat from the waves and ran along the beach calling their names. Nothing. I was starting to lose hope when I spotted a seaweed-covered cave at the far end of the bay, near Stinker's Cove.

I peered into its rancid, dank depths. 'Hello?'

Silence. A moody gull squawked overhead. Then the ripping sound of a match being struck, followed by a croaked syllable.

'Boy?'

I crept to the back of the cave guided by the trembling flame. Mr Baboomski and Zoltan were huddled together, shaking.

'What happened?' I asked.

'Mans come in night, say we must be moving.

I want to tell them to get packed but I grab my tongue. That is how war is started—peoples fighting over pieces of grass. So I am moving trailer to other part of field. Now mans is angry. They says no one can be living anyplace around here—it is rule.'

Typical Smerkinton-Peck, I thought—everyone has to live by his rules.

'Now I is getting angry—they is shoving me and Zoltan so much my foot gets itchy and I have to kick them up the **BABUNSKA**.

PATONK!

'That makes them so crazlepops they is pushing our home into sea.' He sighed. 'Everything is broke.'

I had only ever known Mr Baboomski as a cheerful character, sparkling with life, always ready with a wise word. Now he sat silently; his eyes were dead, his moustache drooping. Zoltan leaned in, licked him under the chin, and gazed at me sadly.

I handed him his hat. 'Escorvia's greatest-ever circus boss can't live in a flipping cave. Come on, it's getting dark—you can stay with us.'

Dad was asleep when we got back to the cottage so I snuck our guests into the garden shed, brought blankets, hot tea, sandwiches, and cheddar puffs, and left them to settle down for the night. Back in the cottage, I crept into Dad's room and pocketed his work keys.

There was something fishy going on up at Spyglass Point and I wanted to get to the bottom of it, starting at the factory.

I stomped through the dimly lit streets, a fiery rage burning inside me. How dare Smerkinton-Peck's men push Mr Baboomski's trailer over the cliff? It may have looked battered and worn but his whole life was crammed in there, and now it was scattered all over the rocks and sand. First thing in the morning I would report this to the police, or Mayor Pudyn—someone important. But right now I needed to find out exactly what Peck was doing up at Spyglass Point that was such a big deal.

Creeping along the darkened corridor at the factory, I started to have doubts. Anger had led me here but now fear was taking hold. What if I was caught? Would Dad be sacked? Would

I be arrested? I was about to turn back when I spotted a light in a distant office. I snuck up to the door and peered through the keyhole.

'So what's the big news, Smerky?' bellowed Mayor Pudyn. 'I'm late for my supper.'

'Keep your voice down,' hissed Smerkinton-Peck. 'Here, read this.'

Pudyn took the folded newspaper and read aloud:

'The food industry is buzzing with news of an exciting competition to find Britain's best regional dishes. An unnamed, food-loving celebrity will travel from Land's End to John o' Groats seeking out local delicacies that: 1. Are new and original; 2. Represent the local community; and 3. Are good for you. The anonymous star will award cash prizes of £1 million to five successful communities to support continued production of their tasty treats.'

'Jolly interesting, I'm sure, but scubbly has been around forever—it's hardly new.'

'Perhaps not but this is,' replied Smerkinton Peck, pulling a slender fish out of a carrier bag and holding it up by its tail in front of the mayor.

'Er, it's a scubbly. Seen 'em before, several in fact, eaten a few in my time, but what has that—'

'Turn off the light.'

'Now really, what on earth is all this—'

'Do it!' snarled Smerkinton-Peck.

The room was plunged into darkness. All I could see was the scubbly, floating in mid-air, glowing a bright, brilliant gold. When the lights came back on, Smerkinton-Peck was still holding up the fish; Mayor Pudyn was hunched forward, his nose a few inches from its sleek body, his glassy eyes staring, his fleshy mouth gaping.

'*Scubblius oriculus*—golden scubbly,' explained Smerkinton-Peck. 'It's a new breed my fishermen discovered during the winter.'

Mayor Pudyn still said nothing: he was in a trance. A glistening trickle of saliva spilled over his lip, dangled for a few seconds then plunged to the floor. When he finally spoke, his voice was husky.

'*Scubblius oriculus*? I never knew such a thing existed.'

Smerkinton-Peck swung the fish sideways, catching the mayor hard across the chops.

THWOCK!

'Of course it doesn't exist, you nincompoop! This is a normal scubbly that has spent some time marinating in a bath of dyed water.'

'Now listen, Smerkinton-Peck,' protested the mayor, rubbing his face. 'Are you suggesting we try and scoop a million quid with a magic, golden fish that doesn't even exist? Surely that's—'

'Listen, Pudyn,' snapped Smerkinton-Peck. He paused, then continued in a gentler tone. 'The scubbly has been good to us but it can't last forever. At the rate we're sucking fish out of the bay, stocks will run out by the end of the year. The factory will have to close, not to mention your restaurant. It's time to cash in our chips on that fish.'

The mayor frowned. 'But Trefuggle Bay without scubbly is like, well, chips without fish—the livelihood of everyone in this town depends on it . . . I suppose if we did win we could use the cash to develop some sort of new tourist attraction.'

Smerkinton-Peck's eyes narrowed. 'Or we could split the money 50/50 and make a run for it.'

Pudyn's pickled-onion eyes bulged. 'But I'm the mayor—I couldn't possibly . . .'

'My dear old friend'—Smerkinton-Peck slipped his arm around Pudyn's shoulders—'you've served this town selflessly for years.' The mayor puffed out his gut and belched softly. 'You deserve a well-earned retirement. Picture yourself sailing off to the Bahamas, in your new yacht . . .'

The glazed expression returned to Mayor Pudyn's face. Another shiny spit bubble dangled from his open mouth.

'. . . your good lady wife sunning herself on deck.'

Pudyn winced and belched again. 'So let me get this straight. We invite this mysterious celebrity here to sample a plate of golden scubbly and chips . . .'

'Already done,' said Smerkinton-Peck smugly. 'Trefuggle Bay will be their first port of call after Land's End. We'll hold a ScubblyFest—music, dancing, prizes for the best fish costume, that sort of thing, to prove how much scubbly represents the local community.'

'Ah!' said Pudyn. 'But what about the third

point? The tasty product has to be good for you.'

'I've thought of that.' Smerkinton-Peck looked even smugger. 'We'll say that golden scubbly has extra-high levels of fish oil; it's a super-food with proven rejuvenating qualities! On the day, we'll bring out some doddery old pensioner, feed them a mouthful, and sit back while they leap around, bursting with health and vitality.'

'But where do we find an old codger willing to play ball?' asked Mayor Pudyn, scratching his bald dome.

'We don't, you fathead,' snapped Smerkinton-Peck. 'Piers will dress up as an old man; Hubert can introduce him as his poor old granddad. Bingo! No one will doubt the word of a child.'

'Hmm.' Pudyn stroked his chins. 'I'm still not sure about this, Smerky—it sounds pretty risky. What if someone finds out?'

'They won't—we'll dye the fish in a closed part of the factory. I've even taken the precaution of fencing off Spyglass Point—we don't want anyone snooping down on our business through that telescope. There was

126

some old tramp squatting in the fields up there but my men soon saw him off. The point is, this whole scam only needs to work long enough to get this famous chump to cough up the cash. While everyone's raving about the amazingly tasty and healthy golden scubbly, we'll scoop the million quid and leave those suckers in our wake.'

The mayor puffed out his cheeks. 'Pity about the scubbly,' he said, rubbing his bulbous belly and licking his moist, ketchup-red lips. 'So many happy memories.'

Smerkinton-Peck grinned wolfishly. 'Don't worry about that stinky old fish—we're going to make a killing.'

Back at home I took some hot chocolate down to the shed and told Mr Baboomski the whole story.

He sighed. 'Why is mans always full of

greedings and grabbings? Don't they see: in life, you only gets what you gives.'

I reddened with shame.

'Listen, Mr Baboomski, about the other day, you were trying to help and I was really rude—I'm sorry. It's just, being down here . . . I miss my old home and friends and my mum's miles away, and my dad's, well, miles away too most of the time . . . if it wasn't for you and Zoltan I . . . I guess what I'm trying to say is that I really value our friendship.'

I swallowed a mouthful of hot chocolate to loosen the lump in my throat. Zoltan, who had been snoozing in the corner of the shed, stirred, gazed at me sleepily, then came and rested her head on my lap. Mr Baboomski sipped his hot chocolate and frowned.

'Mmm, **SKABOONKY**. Is that razonkleberries I am tasting?'

'There's a massive bush of them growing in the car park behind the Jolly Scubbly. I'm pretty sure they're not poisonish.'

He chuckled. 'You is learning all the tricks.' He stared into his mug for a while then took out his hankie, blew his honker, and dabbed his eyes.

'Are you OK, Mr Baboomski?'

'I is,' he replied huskily. 'I am happy sad. I am feeling shames that trailer gets busted up and all my bobs and bits is floating away in sea. But at same time I am filling up with some joys because here'—he waved his mug around in the air—'we have builded something so big and strong it can never be sinked.'

I looked around the shed. 'What's that?'

'A friend ship.'

CRAZLEPOPS KOPPLETOPS

The following morning as we walked into town, I suggested going to the police about Smerkinton-Peck and Pudyn's scheme.

'These mens is boss of this place,' said Mr Baboomski with a sigh. 'No one will believe boy and stupido old man.'

'Hey! You're not stupid!'

'I is. If I wasn't such a dinglebrain, Zoltan would be nibbling green grasses in Ireland now.'

When we got to Saint Scubbly's, he shambled off to the kitchens while I headed for Mrs Pudyn's office.

'Fighting again, Watkinsssss—don't deny it . . . saw it with my own eyesssss.' She was hissing like a turbo-charged kettle coming to the boil. 'And leaving the school premisesssss without permisssssion . . . a month's detention . . . dismissssssed.'

After lunch I wandered into the kitchen and walked into a whirlwind of excited activity. When she saw me, Mrs Brown pulled a cross face.

'Well, I think it's disgusting.'

'Eh?' Mr Baboomski looked up from a large bowl, his moustache frosty with ice cream. 'Are you crazlepops? I think it's **SKABOONKY!**'.

'Not the ice cream, you barmpot—I'm talking to Tom about those men wrecking your trailer. It's disgraceful. Spyglass Point should be open to all—it's a very special place, means a lot to some folk.' Mrs Brown's sea-green eyes blazed through her thick glasses.

'I know,' I said. 'I just wish there was something we could do.'

'Well, for starters, Mr Bambyboomyski and that goat of his are coming to stay with me. I've plenty of space.'

He grinned toothily. He was starting to look a little bit more like his old self. 'That was for starters, now try this for puds.' He held out an ice-cream cone. 'I makes Mrs Brown some hot chocolate, and she nearly yums her head off. Then she is zootzing around bonging pots and pans; everything is boshing and sploshing together: milk, chocolate, scubblies, herbies from my hat. Watching her scootling round the kitchen makes my eyes go seasick.'

Now scubbly, goat's milk, herbs, and chocolate are an unlikely combination but then again so were Mr Baboomski and Mrs Brown, and they worked together brilliantly. The best thing about the ice cream was the surprise wedged halfway down the cone: a koppletop. Just as you were getting over the shock of the icy, salty, fishy, creamy, herby chocolate—WHOAH!—a honey bomb exploded in your mouth.

I started laughing. 'This tastes unbelievable!' Mrs Brown grinned. 'Mr Bambyboomyski was a bit down when he come in this morning but he's full of beans now!' She bustled off into the storeroom.

'Talking about beans,' said Mr Baboomski, 'and pineapple and corny beef and creamy fudge and ketchup, we is getting busy with other flavours. First Mrs Brown is accidentally chucking some raspberries into chicken soup. Then we slops that into ice-cream mixer with some herbies. She holds out spoon. "Try!" she say. "OK, but I'm over here!" I say. I tries. Well. It is disgustingly delicious. Chicken licken tutti frutti! **SKABOONKY!** I say, "Mrs Brown, be giving me high fives!" She slaps me around chops quite hard. (She really can't see for toffee.)

'Talking about chops and toffee, next we is slinging together some sticky spongey pudding and porky casserole. Chewie stewie sundae! It tastes so good I nearly patoof myself. "High fives!" shouts Mrs Brown and flattens my honker.'

Mrs Brown reappeared carrying a bowl of mushy peas, a plate of chopped liver, and a jar of marmalade.

'Right, what's next? I haven't had this much fun in years!' she chuckled. 'Ooh, I feel quite giddy! We're a good team, me and him: I'm half blind and he's half daft.'

'I is also feeling quite giddyish,' muttered Mr Baboomski. 'Too many high fives.'

After school, Zoltan, Mr Baboomski, and I went back to the beach below Spyglass Point to see if we could salvage anything from the wrecked trailer. The tide had claimed most of his meagre possessions but we found some clothes, including a soggy clown outfit, the stilts, and a rather dented blonkipump. The sight of these few, precious things scattered in the wet sand and slimy seaweed made my blood boil.

Mr Baboomski found his battered old frying pan, lit a fire, and started fishing.

'The sea is full of food,' he said, admiring the scubbly dangling from his line. 'Is plenty for all if we only takes what we needs.' He looked over at the factory and shook his head. Some people is full of greedings—they want to stuff themselves with monies. But tell me, boy—can you eat a coin sandwich? No, is too crunchy.'

'Speaking of coins,' I said, 'what about your savings from the kitchen job? Don't tell me they've been lost at sea as well.'

He came and sat down next to me.

'It got spended.' He reached into his coat, pulled out a beautiful silver case, and handed it to me. 'Is present. I buyed it after we had some grumplings the other day, to show we is still friends. Look, I carve your name on front with blade.'

I traced my finger over the three letters, skilfully etched onto the surface of the smooth metal: B.O.Y.

'Open,' he said eagerly. 'Real present is hiding.'

Inside the case, lying on a bed of red velvet, was a tuft of brilliant white hairs, artfully woven together and held in place by a twist of wire. I clipped it to the underside of my nose.

'Perfect—you looks like the dog's dinner!' he said proudly. 'You can ride goat, walk on stilts, do jugglings—you is real proper circus boy now, part of family!' Zoltan ambled up and gave me a slobbery lick, drenching the twirly points of my new moustache.

'That's the best present I've ever had. But what about your tickets to Ireland?'

'Is no probs—soon I earn more coins and then, my old friend'—he patted Zoltan's shaggy neck—'we gets you back home.'

HOW TO MAKE A MEMORY MOUSETARCH

You will needs:

- A hairy friend—goat is best, or horse, maybe dog (not cat, too grumplish).
- Some snippers.
- A koppletop.
- A hat.
- A flute.
- A smart coat.

Please be doing this:

- Take off smart coat and hang it on a coat dangler.
- Feed koppletop to friend and pat them on head.

- Now play softie tune on flute (nothing too tooty, must be full of relaxings).

- Carefully be snippering some snippets from tail or mane or other place with spare hairs.

- Collect snippets in hat (take off first).

- Be weaving hairs together into an imaginary design (this is fiddlish part—poke tongue out of corner of mouth to help you concentrates).

- Put on smart coat. Now coat dangler is free, twist piece of wire off the end to make a curly clip.

- Now be sliding clip into weaved-up hairs (this also quite trickyish—remember to poke tongue).

- Close eyes, pat friend, and think of happy times.

- Now sprinkle these onto mousetarch.
- Is ready! Clip onto honker.
- Take on world.

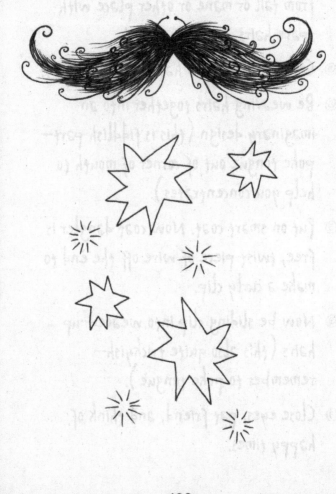

While we ate I gazed out to sea, a confusing mix of emotions washing over me. First there was joy—Mr Baboomski actually rated my circus skills! Then guilt—he had spent his savings on me, they would never get to Ireland at this rate, my Special Project to get them there was failing. Then some sadness—if he did scrape together enough money to move on, I would really miss them both. And finally, as I glanced across at the grey factory, anger. Mr Baboomski's whole life story had been tipped into the sea just because some rich, greedy tripesters were grasping for more money. In a few days' time, Smerkinton-Peck and Pudyn would be sailing off into the sunset having conned some mystery celebrity out of £1 million. It just wasn't right.

'I just wish I could do something about all this.' I sighed. 'I feel so helpless.'

'Just remember, boy, you are only small but you are strong; maybe not here, like Petrov,' he said, pointing at my arms, 'but up here and in here.' He tapped a finger on my forehead and then banged my chest with his fist. 'Trusting me—you can do anything you wants. Now get stuffed.'

He rolled a handful of koppletops onto my plate. Soon I was jumping and hopping all over the place, giggling like a crazlepop.

'Whoah! These have got ice cream inside! This one's—mmmm!—frozen chicken tikka trifle, and what's this? Yikes! Frosted marshmallow bolognaise! These are amazing!'

Mr Baboomski grinned. 'Me and Mrs Brown is getting busy in the kitchen.'

My tastebuds were tingling, my mind was whirring; I felt energized, bursting with life.

'Doctors should prescribe koppletops,' I laughed. 'I reckon they must be good for you . . .'

I stopped. My brain was trying to tell me something. I looked down at the soggy clown outfit, the stilts, and the dented blonkipump, then over at Zoltan who was mucking about in the shallows, trying to catch waves.

Mr Baboomski eyed me quizzically. 'What is up, boy?'

'I don't know . . . it's like there's something right in front of me, something that could be really great, but I can't quite see what it is.'

'Try shutting eyes,' he replied. 'It helps you see.'

SOMETIMES THE ONLY WAY TO SEE IN THE DARK IS TO SHUT YOUR EYES

Man is a dinglebrain. He never learns lesson. I wants to be here so you must go! Clearing off, be scattered, get packed! Since time begins is same story—mans is fighting and pushing and shoving over pieces of grass. For why? What do you get in the end? Nothing but a big bucket full of sad.

When there is war in Escorvia, everything gets lost: homes, friends, smiles, laughings, Pappys. Night falls and can't get up. Everything goes dark—you can't see where to puts your feets to move forward. Grandpappy's heart is breaked when Pappy not come home. He say to me, 'Listen boy, circus is sitting on your shoulder now—you is the captain, you must keep Baboomski name alive.'

'But Grandpappy,' I is saying, 'what do I do? Escorvia is too gloomish—we is living in shadows.'

He say, 'Sometimes the only way to see in the dark is to shut your eyes.'

Then he is having his last sleep.

For longest times I is lying awake at night but not because I am remembering Madame Zootzer's story about the clock that never ticked. I is filled up with worries about how to keep the circus alive. How can we do a show with a couple of clowns and a tired, old horse? I cannot think—my head is too jumblish. So I takes deep breath and shuts my eyes. First everything is fuzzy but then slowly I start to see it ... a new circus show that takes the war and kicks it up the **BABUNSKA**; takes the darkness and chases it away with light and laughings. But how does it work?

The next day we comes to market and I is seeing two beautiful goats, snuffling in the snow. Hey bongo! Before you can do a blink, I am seeing the show that will bring Escorvia out of nightmare!

The peoples will be getting happiness and laughter and in return I gets the chance to be circus boss like Pappy and Grandpappy. Everyone is winning!

HYPNOGOAT

I closed my eyes and tried to steady my racing thoughts. It took a while but gradually my mind began to clear: something was coming; soon it was so close I could almost smell it! SPLOOPSH! I felt a long, sandpapery tongue slide across my forehead.

'Urrggh, Zoltan what the—?'

She fixed me with a dreamy look. And then something truly weird happened. As I stared back at her, I began to see all these blurry pictures swirling in the deep pools of her sleepy eyes: Mayor Pudyn and Mr Smerkinton-Peck dancing around, as golden fish and coins rained down; I saw myself on a stage dressed as a clown; then Mr Baboomski appeared, firing koppletops from the blonkipump, and, finally, Zoltan drifted into the scene, no longer brilliant white but gleaming gold!

All this swirled and whirled around in those eyes the colour of liquid honey holding me in a trance. Zoltan blinked, lowered a sleepy eyelid and trotted away.

'I'VE GOT IT!' I shouted.

Mr Baboomski, who was squatting by a rock pool rinsing off his frying pan, nearly fell into the sea. 'Eh! What do you got, boy?'

'A plan. An insane plan, a bonkers plan, a plan so flipping crazy . . . it might just work.'

'Hey, bongo! That sounds like a great plan!' Mr Baboomski was swishing his frying pan in the air like a giant table-tennis bat. 'I say: let's do it! And then I say: what is we doing?!'

'For starters we're going to show everyone what evil tripesters Pudyn and Smerkinton-Peck really are—we'll make sure that they don't get their grasping mitts on that million pounds. Then we will enter the competition ourselves, showing off the best Trefuggle Bay really has to offer: an amazing new, local delicacy that's as delicious as it is good for you. We can use some of the winnings to send you and Zoltan to Ireland in style.'

'I love this plan! I don't get it but I loves it!'

'Don't worry, I'll explain everything but I need your help, and Zoltan's. Would you guys be up for one last big performance?'

He stood up and slipped the frying pan into his overcoat. His hair was straggly, his eyes danced, his teeth were chaotic, his clothes were shabby, he had a large kitchen utensil in his pocket; when a strong gust of wind blew in from the sea, his moustache began to swing at half-mast. But at that moment, standing there in the fiery glow of the setting sun, to my eyes, Mr Baboomski looked like a superhero.

'Boy, you heards what Mrs Brown says,' he declared, throwing back his shoulders and sticking out his chin. 'I is half daft! Of course we will help.'

'Brilliant! OK, we need to get cracking, we've got a show to rehearse! We're going to need the stilts, the blonkipump, a bit of clowning around, and a whole load of koppletops!'

I ran down to the water's edge and yelled at the crashing waves.

'**SKABOONKY**!'

THINGS GET A BIT FRUITY

Trefuggle Bay was bathed in sunshine for the ScubblyFest. Word had spread about the mystery celebrity and the £1 million prize; in no time the town and beaches were packed. As Dad and I made our way down to the seafront, a huge fish bombed past on a bicycle, a tiny dog with a giant dorsal fin was in hot pursuit, yipping its head off. Behind them a bearded old man wearing a flowing tunic made of shiny, silver scales swayed by, banging a drum, leading a conga line of dancing kids dressed in crazy, scubblyish costumes. Overhead the gulls were going beserk, especially when Mayor Pudyn cruised by in his giant inflatable scubbly, booming at the crowds below through his megaphone.

'Don't forget the big event tonight, folks, down by the fish factory! Speaking of fish, why not head for the Golden Scubbly? Free pickled egg for every accompanied child!'

With the sun sinking, Mayor Pudyn and his megaphone drove the crowds down the beach to the factory. The glass scubbly tank was shrouded in a red velvet curtain. Above it there was a raised platform with three thrones: one each for the mayor and Mr Smerkinton-Peck, the other for the star guest. In front of the tank, rows of benches were slowly filling up. I sat down with Dad, near the end of a row, and started to feel a bit nervish. If anything went wrong with my plan—and plenty could go wrong—I would have quite an audience.

The mayor landed his floating fish on the beach, scrambled gracelessly out of the basket, and stepped up onto the stage. It was show-time.

'Citizens of Trefuggle Bay, beloved visitors, we are gathered here today to witness something truly magical: the unveiling of an astonishing new delicacy that will send shockwaves through the realms of oceanography and gastronomy and will, I am sure, impress our illustrious guest'—the mayor checked his watch anxiously—'who is due to arrive any minute.'

An expectant hush fell over the crowd.

People craned their necks back towards the high street, looking for a limousine. Others peered up at the sky or out to sea, scanning the horizon for signs of a helicopter or speedboat. Several minutes passed; a restless, fidgety murmuring in the crowd slowly became an excited buzz.

'Look!'

'Where?'

'Up there, drifting across the bay!'

'What is it?'

'It looks like . . . no, it can't be!'

'It is, it's a flipping great pineapple!'

All eyes turned to the skies watching the mammoth, spikey blob floating serenely towards the beach. I could just make out the outline of two people standing in a basket dangling beneath the ginormous fruit. It drifted gracefully to the ground, landing on the sand with a dull thud. Someone vaulted out of the basket—a tall figure in a cream shirt and pink and white striped trousers. His wrinkled face shone with a healthy glow, his silver hair was scraped back into a long plait. A diamond stud glinted in each earlobe and a long, pearly-white shark's tooth swung on a chain beneath his unbuttoned shirt. He looked like a really cool old person—how weird is that? The crowd went bananas.

'It's Dr Smoothy!'

'Give us a wave!'

'Sing us a song!'

'Yeah! How about "Gooseberry Fool for Love"!'

'No, let's have: "I Lost My Heart Down the Back of Your Sofa"!'

' "Mangos by Moonlight"!'

'How about: "Don't Start Juggling With Our Snuggling"!'

Dr Smoothy arched an eyebrow in their direction to huge applause then helped a second figure out of the basket. It was Mum, dressed in a smart business suit, carrying a shiny, silver briefcase. My first instinct was to rush over to her but I couldn't: there was some serious work ahead and I didn't want any distractions. Next to me, Dad was sitting bolt upright, a storm of emotions raging on his face: first he looked happy, then cross, then confused and then, finally, when Mum spotted us and waved in our direction, a bit, well, soppy.

Dr Smoothy addressed the crowd. 'What

a peach of a reception! Good people, I am honoured to visit your beautiful town and I look forward to sampling the exciting new delicacy it has to offer.'

Behind his back, I spotted Smerkinton-Peck and the mayor exchanging sly winks.

'I'm putting my money where my mouth is,' continued the star guest, becoming serious. 'Investing in sustainable, local produce is the future—transporting food long distances in trucks and planes is choking up the atmosphere with fug and fumes. It's time we showed this old planet of ours a little love.'

The crowd whooped in agreement. Mum handed him a raspberry-pink ukulele.

'I'd like to perform a song from my latest album. It's called: "You Melted My Heart Like a Polar Ice Cap". Do join in the chorus.'

. . . acid rain, you're such a pain;
CO_2, I'm coming for you;
Greenhouse gas, you can kiss my . . .

The crowd knew every word. When all was quiet and Dr Smoothy had taken his seat on the central throne, Mayor Pudyn bounced onto the stage.

'Ladies, gents, most honoured guest, it is time to unveil a wondrous, new, and original taste sensation; a local speciality entirely unique to this little corner of Cornwall. He stepped forward to the edge of the stage, produced a large pair of scissors, and snipped: the velvet curtain surrounding the tank fell to the floor to reveal a golden ribbon of scubbly, unfurling itself in the shimmering water.

'Behold: GOLDEN SCUBBLY!' boomed the mayor.

The crowd gasped in amazement. Up on the stage, Dr Smoothy rose from his throne and gawped at the tank. Mayor Pudyn raised his megaphone but, for once, spoke softly.

'My dear people, you can say that "I was there that day"; you will be the envy of thousands of visitors flocking to Trefuggle Bay to feast their eyes on this wondrous specimen—not to mention their bellies, down at the Golden Scubbly (free pickled onion for the under-fives, weekdays after 9 p.m.).'

The mayor could have said anything he liked; no one was listening. They were hypnotized by the golden fish, caught in a spell: hook, line, and sinker. A fatly contented expression spread across his oily face. He ran his tongue around his ketchup-red lips, his glassy pickled-onion eyes bulged: you could almost see the pound signs spinning in them. He nodded at Smerkinton-Peck—their carefully planned performance had proved a big hit.

Little did they know, the show was only just beginning.

IF YOU FALL ON YOUR BABUNSKA, JUST BOUNCE BACK UP AGAIN

Soon the goat show is faming all over Escorvia. One day I am getting letter in fancy envelope—Queen Anna is wanting a show at the palace! All the poshest hoitily toitily peoples is invited, I is getting nervish. Then I is reminding myself about what Pappy used to say before each show: 'Don't be scary—what is the worst can happen? If you fall on your **BABUNSKA**, just bounce back up again!'

So I is stepping out onto the big fancy stage. My knees is knocking, my gootle is all swirly. Crowd is waiting. They looks a bit grumplish. So I shouts, 'Don't make a frown—

show is in town! (Now where is clown?)'.
Then Clonky creeps up and is hoofing me up
the **BABUNSKA**. I rolls over, throw hat
in air, and catch it on my foot. Crowd starts
cheerzing like nutcrackers. Skaboonky!

At end of show when crowd is all
clapped out, Queen Anna is calling me up
to her throne. Now my guts is dancing again,
jiggling and joggling around like Nipsy after
too much beer. I look at Queen: her skin
is like snow, her eyes sparkle like jewels,
her teeth is all in the right places. She is
as delicate as a butterfly, as graceful as a
swan—she is like a butter swan. She smiles
elegantly. Finally she speak: 'Hey, bongo!
I am loving your show. I laughs so much I
nearly patoof myself!'

'Thank you, your highest-ness,' I say, turning purple as a plum.

'No, let me be thanking you.' She look serious, she puts down her pipe. 'Our country has been ugly for too long because of these stupid warrings. Your show makes it beautiful again. Please be accepting this.'

She hands me a beautiful silvery case; inside is the Escorvian Medal of Honour. On top of case in curly, swirly letters it say:

BABOOMSKI—
KING OF THE CIRCUS

I am filling up with pride, I have chunks in my throat.

'Thanking you, your Magic Sea,' I says. 'I accept this great honour for me, my Grandpappy, and my Pappy.'

And I slide the silvery case deep, deep into my coat, next to my heart.

LIFE HAS A MILLION MINUTES BUT ONLY A FEW MOMENTS

Everyone was so fixated on the tank, that no one noticed me slip out of my seat and nip around to the back of the factory where I found Zoltan and an excitable Mr Baboomski.

'So good so far, boy! Now get clobbered, no time to lose!' He helped me clamber into the baggy clown outfit and jumbo shoes, dusted my face with white powder, smeared a blob of red paint on each cheek, and jammed a glittery bowler hat on my head.

I reached into the deep, baggy pocket and felt the cool, smooth surface of the silver case. My hands were shaking so much I couldn't even open it. I was about to step out in front of a whole crowd of people, not to mention everyone at school. What if they laughed? Worse still, what if they didn't? Mr Baboomski gently took the case, opened it, and held up the moustache.

'Boy, you earned this. Never forget to remember who you is: you is the prince of circus tricks.'

The snowy white strands on the moustache stood up in the sea breeze, just like the hairs on the back of my neck.

'Don't be scary,' he said softly. 'What is worst that can happen? If you fall on your **BABUNSKA**, just bounce back up again.'

'But I don't know if I'm ready for this.'

'You was born ready.' He tapped his knuckles on my forehead and chest. 'You is strong up in here and in there. You know that I know that you know that you can do this. Life has a million minutes but only a few moments. Now is your moment.'

I took a deep breath and clipped on my moustache.

'How do I look?' I asked nervously.

Mr Baboomski grew serious, and his cross eyes became misty. He placed his hands on my shoulders and looked me straight in the ears.

'You look like a flipping clown.'

My heart swelling with pride, I scampered

off as fast as the baggy pants and giant shoes would let me and made it to the back of the stage just in time to see Mayor Pudyn place a steaming plate of golden scubbly in front of Dr Smoothy. Meanwhile staff from his restaurant were handing out samples to the crowd. Without taking his eyes off the tank, the rock star broke off a chunk of golden fish and ate it. His eyebrows arched approvingly.

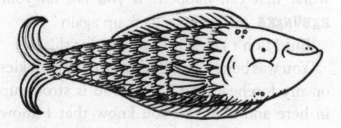

'Mmmm! Utterly delicious, Mayor Pudyn, and clearly a unique local delicacy . . . but is it really good for you?'

'My dear Dr Smoothy,' purred the mayor, stroking his bloated belly, 'you have no idea. This rare and scrumptious fish puts the "mega" into omega 3! It's a natural tonic—allow me to demonstrate.'

He clicked his fingers. Hubert lumbered up the steps onto the stage accompanied by Piers, shuffling pathetically, hunched into a large overcoat with a hat pulled down to his beaky nose, and a false, grey beard hiding his chin.

Hubert grinned at the expectant crowd then gawped at his father.

'Go on then, lad,' Pudyn muttered, fixing him with a steely glare.

'Oh yeah.' Hubert scratched his generous backside. 'Er, this 'ere is my old granddad. He is . . . er . . . old and can't really do nuffink. I wonder what would 'appen if he eated some golden scubbly?'

Mayor Pudyn leapt forward. 'Let's find out, shall we?' he boomed, posting a morsel of fish between Piers's fake whiskers.

Hubert's 'old granddad' rose slowly from his crooked stoop. He carefully stretched out his arms. He hopped lightly on one foot, then the other. Then he started breakdancing.

'Don't overdo it, lad,' hissed Mayor Pudyn through clenched teeth. Out loud he boomed, 'Well, folks, there you have it: golden scubbly—a delicious, local delicacy that's seriously good for you!'

Dr Smoothy stepped forward and raised his hands to silence the cheering crowd.

'I have visited the four corners of the globe and eaten many unusual and delicious foods. But this'—he gestured down at the tank full of darting, golden daggers—'this is quite unbelievable.'

He stroked his beard elegantly, using the long, smooth shark's fang dangling around his neck as a toothpick, then signalled to Mum, who passed him the silver briefcase.

'Mayor Pudyn, I am pleased to award your fine town £1 million to help support the continued production of this sumptuous and intriguing local dish.'

The crowd roared. Mayor Pudyn bowed, took the briefcase, and glanced over his shoulder at Mr Smerkinton-Peck, receiving a satisfied smirk in return. Their evening was going swimmingly. Time to pull the plug.

My heart raced, my knees were like jelly. Could I really do this? Then Mr Baboomski's voice drifted into my mind: 'Trusting me—you can do anything you wants . . . You is now the prince of circus tricks.' I twirled my moustache and ran up the steps onto the stage, tripping and slipping in the floppy shoes.

A sea of expectant faces swam before me.

I felt sick and dizzy. Glancing across the stage I saw Piers, still dressed up as the old man, smirking nastily; an anxious-looking Mayor Pudyn was starting to head my way. It was now or never. I took a deep breath—the warm, goaty aroma from my moustache reminded me of that first terrifying ride up the cliffs, my head buried in Zoltan's shaggy neck, and how proud I had been when I reached the top.

'My goat's got no nose!' I announced, as loud as my shaking voice would allow.

An endless silence followed. Finally, a voice from the crowd answered. 'How does it smell?'

'Terrible.'

The ancient joke drew a polite ripple of laughter; I pressed on before Pudyn could interrupt.

'And boy, is it lazy! Aren't goats supposed to charge around and butt things? The only butt that thing cares about is the one it sits on all day!'

More laughter. I was holding their attention, just.

'Seriously, folks, talk about a dumb animal—I can't even get any milk out of it. It's udderly useless!'

The crowd groaned and laughed. I couldn't believe it—they were actually enjoying the show! Mayor Pudyn wasn't. He bounced onto the stage, his dome-shaped head purple with rage.

'Right then, young man, that's quite enough. This is a private area, move along please.'

Grumplish mutterings rose from the crowd. I ignored the mayor and addressed Dr Smoothy.

'But I haven't finished—our special guest hasn't sampled Trefuggle Bay's other great delicacy yet.'

The rock legend raised a quizzical eyebrow, a woman in the front row swooned.

'A bit of competition, eh? I like it! Come on, Mayor Pudyn, step aside, let's see what the kid has to offer.'

There was a buzz of approval from the crowd. The mayor gave me a sour look and waddled off the stage.

'Right, where was I? Oh yes, trying to milk my hopeless goat. I'm really getting cheesed off. Stop me if I'm bleating on, but if you ask me, that dumb animal needs a good hoof up the **BABUNSKA**.'

The crowd stopped laughing and started to

mutter and whisper—they had spotted Zoltan creeping up the steps onto the stage.

'Look out, it's behind you!' shouted a kid in the front row.

'Come off it,' I shouted back. 'I'm not falling for that old one.'

Soon all the kids in the crowd were pointing, yelling their heads off. Eventually I turned around and jumped theatrically at the sight of the advancing goat.

'Now then.' I raised my hands. 'You're acting like a kid.' Zoltan snorted. 'Hey! Don't get gruff with me,' I scolded, edging backwards, unclipping the cape from my clown suit and holding it up in front of me.

Zoltan lowered her head and charged. The crowd gasped and screamed. I stood my ground but as she reached me, I darted to one side, sweeping aside the cape like a bullfighter, and grabbed a horn, heaving myself onto her back. As the crowd whooped and cheered, I rode Zoltan around the stage as she kicked and bucked like mad.

'Help! Someone make it stop!' I shouted.

'OK, keep your hairs on!' Mr Baboomski tottered onto the stage on stilts, eyes rolling, moustache twirling, purple smoke pouring from his top hat. He pulled the blonkipump from his coat and dropped a koppletop into the end.

'Here boy, try one of these—that will do the tricks!'

Pop! He fired the koppletop in my direction. As it looped across the stage, Zoltan leapt gracefully into the air. I twirled my moustache, raised my bowler hat, leaned back, and **PLOP!** the tasty treat fell into my gaping mouth. The kids in the front row cheered so loud they must have nearly patoofed themselves.

'Wow, that was delicious!' I yelled. 'Sticky toffee black pudding!'

'Was not for you, dinglebrain!' shouted Mr Baboomski, reloading the blonkipump.

POP! POP! POP! POP! POP!

A volley of koppletops sailed through the air. I caught the first, then the second and the third . . . soon I was juggling all five.

'No, no—stop horsing around, you nutcracker! Feed the goat!' Mr Baboomski yanked off his hat in frustration. An angry-looking seagull flapped out.

'Speak for yourself, birdbrain!' I yelled back,
as Zoltan galloped between his stilts.

POP! POP! POP! POP! POP!

The crowd roared. Riding a wild goat, whilst juggling and telling bad jokes . . . they'd never seen a show like it! As I zoomed past, I caught quick glimpses of the bemused group huddled at the side of the stage. Pudyn's glassy eyes bulged, Smerkinton-Peck looked aghast—what was happening to their cunning plan? Hubert looked even more gormless than usual, quite an achievement; next to him Piers, still in the ridiculous 'old man' disguise, was glowering with spite and envy—how come the crowd were cheering for this stupid clown and not him? Dr Smoothy seemed to be enjoying the show, one debonair eyebrow raised in amusement.

I flung the koppletops into the air and gave Zoltan the signal we had practised—two gentle taps on her flanks. She skidded to a halt right at the very edge of the stage, in front of the fish tank, and leaned her head back lazily letting the tasty treats drop into her mouth one by one. I looked out across a sea of faces, full of bright eyes and happy smiles. Our show was a hit! Now for the grand finale . . .

I shouted over to Mr Baboomski, 'OK, scaredy pants, it's safe to come down now.'

'My pants isn't scary,' he replied huffily. 'OK, here I come—hold this, mister!'

He'd dropped the blonkipump down to Mayor Pudyn who caught it, his pickled-onion eyes still boggling with confusion. At that moment, just as we had planned, I dropped a Thunder Bomb down the baggy trouser leg of my clown suit and stamped on it.

Zoltan wobbled for a few dramatic seconds then fell forward into the tank, a dead weight sinking like a stone, scattering the golden scubbly in all directions.

LADIES AND GENTS—
PLEASE GET STUFFED!

A stunned silence fell over the crowd. Eventually a small, tearful voice broke the spell.

'Mummy, why did the fat man shoot the nice horsey?'

Mayor Pudyn gawped helplessly at the blonkipump in his hands. Boos echoed around the bay. Mr Baboomski sidled over, handed me the stilts, and muttered, 'OK, boy, let's turn this boozing into cheerzing.'

'WAIT!' I shouted, silencing the crowd. 'I think it's OK—look, she's swimming back to the surface!'

I lowered the stilts carefully into the tank side by side, giving Zoltan a ramp to walk up out of the water—just like that day in the fields when she had first helped me find my balance. On the day of the big performance Zoltan was a picture of poise and grace, strutting up the stilts onto centre stage and standing in front of the crowd like a magnificent statue. A magnificent golden statue.

It didn't take people long to work out what was going on.

'Hang on, that goat was white before it fell in the tank!'

'Hey! Those fish aren't really golden— there's something in the water!'

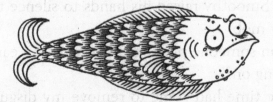

'It's a con! Boo! Boo!'

Mayor Pudyn tried desperately to regain control of the situation.

'I can assure you these are golden scubbly with special health-giving properties. Remember how they cured that poor old man.'

I walked across the stage to where the boys were standing. Piers pulled the brim of his hat down even further.

'You wouldn't dare, Watkins,' he hissed. His

mean, beady eyes looked me and up and down. 'What do you look like?' he sneered.

'I look like a flipping clown.' **HOOF!** My jumbo shoe printed itself on his **BABUNSKA**. As he stumbled forward, his hat fell off, and the false beard slipped away.

'Oi! That's not an old man, it's a kid!'

'No wonder he could breakdance!'

'Well, this is a fishy business!'

'Boo! Boo!'

Dr Smoothy raised his hands to silence the angry mob.

'Can someone please explain what on earth is going on?'

The time had come to remove my disguise too; I started to feel really nervous again. I took a deep breath, inhaling the reassuring smell of goat. I'd come this far, what was the worst that could happen now? If I fell on my **BABUNSKA**, I'd just bounce back up again. I picked up Mayor Pudyn's megaphone, took off my glittery hat and unclipped my moustache.

I spotted Dad in the crowd; he was staring straight at me, his mouth frozen into a perfect 'O'. I glanced over at Mum; she looked ready to patoof herself.

'Um, hello, everyone. As you can see, there's actually no such thing as golden scubbly; it was all just a scam dreamed up by the mayor and Mr Smerkinton-Peck to get their hands on a million quid.' The crowd muttered disapprovingly. 'Thanks to them, the real scubbly won't exist either, soon. This amazing, beautiful fish is being hoovered up by the trawlers and chucked in the deep fat fryers at the Golden Scubbly at such a rate that it's almost extinct.'

Dr Smoothy somehow managed to look horrified, furious, and incredibly stylish all at once. I handed him the megaphone.

'There's clearly fishy business at work here'—he glowered at Pudyn and Smerkinton-Peck—'and I intend to inform the authorities at the earliest opportunity.' He gazed up at the sky looking disappointed, in a dashing sort of way. 'My faith in humanity has suffered today; this has clearly been a wasted journey.'

'Not so fast, Dr Smoochy—please pop this in cake-hole.' Mr Baboomski handed him a koppletop.

The legendary rock star took it warily and popped it in his mouth. He gave a little shudder, then he started to chuckle.

'Oh baby, that's good. I've never tasted anything quite so . . .'

'**SKABOONKY**?'

'Exactly! I'm getting fish and banana curry and, ooh, is that really salad cream? Whoah! Give me another!' He started hopping around the stage, flapping his arms like a chicken, laughing his head off. For once Dr Smoothy didn't look so smooth.

Mr Baboomski retrieved the blonkipump from a gaping Mayor Pudyn, loaded it to the brim with koppletops, and aimed it at the crowd. **POP! POP! POP! POP! POP! POP!**

'Ladies and gents—
please get stuffed!'

Soon everyone was scrambling to catch the

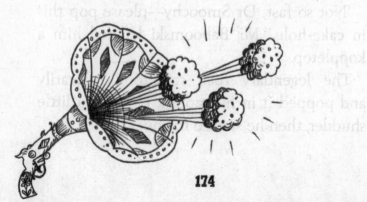

tasty treats raining down from the sky.

'What the—? Tuna cheesecake ripple! Yum!'

'This one's a cheese and pickle sundae!'

'I've got a chilli con apple crumble sorbet!'

When the commotion had died down, a giggling Dr Smoothy said, 'I've never tasted anything quite like it. What is this mind-blowing stuff?'

I lifted the megaphone and looked over at Mr Baboomski and Zoltan; then I spotted Mrs Brown in the crowd, beaming happily in the wrong direction.

'The ice cream is made of all kinds of things: friendship, luck, goat's milk, herbs from the hedgerows, the tiniest pinch of precious scubbly, the best ingredients Trefuggle Bay has to offer . . . all wrapped up in an Escorvian secret. Ice-cream koppletops: a unique local delicacy that's so flipping tasty you can't help laughing—what could be healthier than that?'

The crowd, most of whom were still scoffing koppletops, roared with delight.

Dr Smoothy stepped to the front of the stage.

'My journey to find Britain's finest local dishes has already taken me further than I ever dreamed possible. I've found something new and original that reflects the best of this community, while preserving its natural assets. As for being healthy? I've never felt better—fishy, spicy ice cream! Genius! A worthy winner of a £1 million prize.'

The crowd cheerzed like nutcrackers. Mrs Brown walked onto the stage wheeling a barrowload of koppletops for Mr Baboomski to fire in their direction while Dr Smoothy picked up his ukulele and belted out some fruity numbers. A wild party broke out—wherever you looked people were singing, dancing, and scoffing koppletops. Trefuggle Bay's inaugural ScubblyFest was a huge hit.

Somewhere amidst the chaos I found Mum and gave her a massive hug. Before she could say anything, Dad stumbled through the crowd and, with a cry of 'Doreen!', joined the huddle. Once we had extricated ourselves, Mum eyed us both quizzically. 'So listen, you two, what on earth is going on?'

Dad looked sheepish. 'I have absolutely no idea. I guess I've been so busy with my own problems lately I haven't been around much for you, Tom.' He stared at the floor.

'It's fine, Dad, I understand. Sometimes life is full of confusings, it's hard to know where is what and who is you.'

Mum and Dad exchanged worried glances.

'Look, the whole thing's a long story but first I want you to meet my very special friends.' We weaved through the crowd to where Mr Baboomski was showing off his sparkling goat to a group of star-struck kids.

'Mum, I'd like you to meet Mr Baboomski: Escorvia's greatest ever circus boss. The golden one is Zoltan, Zoltan the Wonder Goat.'

Mum and Dad exchanged another anxious glance.

Mr Baboomski became very serious. He took Mum and Dad by the hand and stared at them intensely. For once his eyes were perfectly still and focused. When he spoke, his voice was hushed but clear.

'Let me tell you this: your boy is clever and brave and kind; he has a big heart and a good noggin. He knows that, in life, doings things is easy, doing the right thing is hard. You has the best boy in the world. You is lucky peoples.'

Mum looked at me, her eyes misting over. 'We is,' she whispered.

Then Mr Baboomski hugged Dad. And Mum hugged Zoltan. And Mrs Brown popped up and, with a cry of 'We did it, Mr Bambyboomyski!', hugged a passing Dr Smoothy, who didn't seem to mind. Soon everyone was getting on like old friends. It was a crazy, perfect end to a perfectly crazy day. Until . . .

'Oi! Oi! Get back here, you tripesters!' shouted Mr Baboomski suddenly, pointing to the beach.

But Mayor Pudyn, Mr Smerkinton-Peck, Piers, and Hubert weren't stopping for anyone. They were heading straight for the giant inflatable scubbly, the mayor leading the way, clutching the silver briefcase full of cash. We set off in pursuit but it was too late. The flipping great fish rose gracefully into the sky and drifted gently away across the sea.

GOATHANGER

The crowd poured down onto the beach, buzzing with excitement—they thought this was all part of the show. Dr Smoothy was rocking with rage, waggling his pink ukulele at the airborne fish.

'Get back here, you scoundrels! You thieves! You eco-vandals!'

He sank to one knee in the sand, his forehead resting stylishly on his clenched fist.

'If only we could pursue them,' he wailed, shaking his head groovily. 'But how? How?'

Mum cleared her throat and nodded towards the humungous floating pineapple parked a little way down the beach.

'Of course, the Fruituador!' Dr Smoothy leapt to his feet and threw some celebratory dance moves. 'Follow me!'

Dr Smoothy, Mum, and Dad raced off down the beach; by the time I arrived with Zoltan and Mr Baboomski the pineapple was already floating several feet off the ground. Mum peered over the side of the basket and threw a rope ladder down to us.

I reached the ladder first but couldn't get a proper grip: it was swinging around too much. Zoltan galloped up and bit down hard on the bottom rung, holding it steady while Mr Baboomski climbed aboard. I was about to follow him when **WHOOSH!** the pineapple suddenly shot skywards. I just had time to grab one of Zoltan's legs as we soared upwards; she gazed down at me dreamily, still happily chewing away on the last rung of the ladder. The rope looked frayed and stringy—one more munch and we would be buried at sea. Up above me Mum, Dad, and Dr Smoothy peered anxiously over the side of the basket. The crowds on the beach gasped.

'Don't worry, boy! I is coming!' yelled Mr Baboomski, hooking his feet into the ladder and swinging upside down. With a sickening **TWANG!** the rope snapped. For one awful split second I felt the gravitational pull of a jumbo goat, and then **AYOOP!** the reassuring clutch of a strong hand around my wrist. Mr

Baboomski was dangling from the end of the ladder at full stretch, Zoltan's horn in one hand, me in the other. A roar of approval and applause rose from the beach.

'Eh! Look, boy!' he shouted triumphantly. 'I is angry bat and you is goat hanger! It remembers me about the time when Clunky and Nipsy gets caught up in Miss Sylvie Starlight's pantaloons . . .'

'Er, Mr Baboomski,' I yelled. 'Could I maybe hear that one later, only I'm patoofing myself a bit down here.'

'No probs, just be climbing up my arm like you is a cheeky monkey. Pieces of cakes!'

But it wasn't pieces of cakes. His coat was so old and smooth I couldn't get a grip on his sleeve; soon I was scrabbling around desperately. Mr Baboomski could see that I was slipping but only had one hand free; his fingers were a dizzying blur as he clutched and grasped at my wrist but it was no good . . .

I was falling, falling, falling . . . sinking faster than a hungry seagull swooping down on a plump, tasty scubbly.

SOMETIMES A BIG PILE OF POOTLE CAN GROW A BEAUTIFUL FLOWER

When Peypa fall down, crowds is boozing and cheerzing—they think this is all part of show. They is leaving big tent full of joyness. I is filling up with sad; my gootle is sinking to my boots. Animal doctor come and is using some fancy words but I know the truth: Peypa's heart is broked; she is full of sad at all the boozing from crowd—it is circus that is sending her for longest sleep.

I just don't gets it—how can something full of happiness be doing something so full of sad? Me and Zoltan is standing there looking down at Peypa, our eyes is getting leakish. I takes out my flute and plays most gloomyish song I knows, it called: Zonko Badonko, Slipperty Slapperty Slonko. Then I is standing there thinking for the longest time until a light bulb blows off in my brain. I can see that war in Escorvia is saddest time—I is losing Pappy and Grandpappy, circus is dying. But this darkest shadow leads to shining light: I is ending up with two lovely goats and a show that gets the whole country cheerzed up. Now I gets it!

Sometimes a big pile of pootle can grow a beautiful flower.

So I is laying my head on Peypa's

softy coat—she is still warm and smelling of goatyness—and I is saying some thankings for the good times and for helping me when I am down in the dump after Pappy and Grandpappy is gone. I wants to keep these rememberings so I am snippering some hairs from her tail to dangle under my honker until the breaths stop coming out of it.

Then I is looking at Zoltan and I is making myself two promisings. First I will be looking after her with greatest care, and second, never again will I be losing a star from the Baboomski circus.

HOME AT LAST

As I plummeted towards the sea I could see the horrified faces staring down at me from the basket above, but the only eyes I really focused on were Zoltan's. I should have been terrified but the sight of those dreamy pools of liquid honey somehow made me feel totally calm: I was drifting gently through the air, coasting slowly downwards to the waves below; as light as a feather, as free as a bird. Zoltan lowered a sleepy eyelid and . . . I stopped falling. I was floating in mid-air, halfway between the sky and the sea. A grumpy seagull darted past, squawking moodily in my ear, bringing me to my senses.

I looked up and saw the spotted hankie knotted to my wrist, one of many hundreds joining me in a stringy lifeline to Mr Baboomski's sleeve far above. He grinned and waved.

'Not times for hanging about, boy! Blow

your honker and get up here. We've got some tripesters to catch!'

Down on the beach, the crowd whooped with glee. This show just got better and better.

By the time I had climbed up the twine of knotted hankies, Mr Baboomski had managed to heave Zoltan onto his back and was climbing up the rope ladder. We fell into the basket exhausted; an ashen-faced Mum started to fuss over me but there wasn't time for all that—the flying scubbly was getting away.

'Can't this thing go any faster?' I asked, looking up at the huge spikey pineapple above us. 'By the way, what is this thing?'

'It's a prototype we developed in Questimu,' explained Mum. 'It's essentially a giant flutuador—although fruituador is probably more accurate. It's made of feather-light wood: one short, sharp boost of hot air gets it airborne, the little flaps catch in the wind, and nature does the rest. As a modern means of transport it's perfect: cheap and environmentally friendly. The skies over Questimu are starting to look like a giant fruit bowl.'

Dad looked at her proudly then

addressed Doctor Smoothy. 'Right, put your fruit down, I mean foot down—we need to catch that fish!'

There was a loud

WHOOSH!

then a fluttering sound, like a squadron of moths attacking a windowpane, as the jumbo fruit floated up and cruised out to sea, creaking and groaning like an old shed on a stormy night.

By the time we had reached the edge of the bay, we had nearly caught the massive floating scubbly. But then what? Far below, down by Stinker's Cove, a noisy mob of gulls was screeching and swooping, fighting for space in a dark, oily slick of sea. A terrible fishy stink filled the air.

'Urgh! This is where they pump out the waste from the factory,' said Dad, holding his nose.

A light bulb blew off in my brain. Pump! Of course!

'Mr Baboomski, pass me the blonkipump!' He pulled it out of his coat. 'Thanks. Now I just need a sharp object . . .'

'Will this do?' Dr Smoothy unhooked the gleaming shark's tooth from the chain around his neck.

I dropped the fang into the trumpet of the blonkipump and took aim at my fishy target. Mr Baboomski placed his hand on my shoulder.

'Remember, boy: don't smell the fear—it stinks! Sniff with your mind!'

I opened my mind and shut my face. I listened to my heart and breathed with my ears. Then I pulled the trigger. **ZING!** The pointy tooth shot through the still evening air and bit right into the heart of the floating fish. There was a loud **POP!**, a fierce hissing sound like Mrs Pudyn on the warpath, then a gentle sigh as the inflatable scubbly crumpled and collapsed into the rotten soup below.

Up in the basket we cheerzed like mad; far away, on the distant beach, the crowd hollered and yelled. This was a show to tell the grandchildren about! Below us, caught in the glare of searchlights from an onrushing fleet of police boats, Mayor Pudyn, still clinging to the silver briefcase, Mr Smerkinton-Peck, Piers, and Hubert were splashing around helplessly in the putrid swamp as swarms of angry gulls pecked mercilessly at their bobbing heads.

Dr Smoothy arched a debonair eyebrow in my direction. 'Peach of a shot, young man. The police will recover the cash and deliver it to the rightful owner. Speaking of which, who is responsible for those amazing little balls of ice-creamy delight I was scoffing earlier?'

'They were created by Mr Baboomski and Mrs Brown, in her kitchen,' I explained. 'We were hoping that she could use some of the winnings to start up production on a larger scale—maybe open an ice-cream place on the seafront.'

'A capital idea,' said Dr Smoothy, peering towards the Golden Scubbly. 'Perhaps she could buy that place—I don't think the current owner will be around to use it. But you said, "some of the winnings" . . . ?'

'Well, the thing is, Mr Baboomski here needs to get his goat back to Ireland, so we thought he could maybe use some of the cash for that.'

I looked over at the old circus boss and felt a lump rising in my throat. He also looked pretty emotional: he was staring out to sea, his cross eyes misty, his moustache quivery.

'Boy,' he said in a croaky, breaking voice,

squinting into the far distance, 'I do it, I really do it! We is nearly there.' He pointed at the horizon. 'Look! We is nearly at Ireland!'

There was a moment's silence, which I broke rather nervously. 'Er, Mr Baboomski?'

'Ja?'

'That's the Scilly Isles.'

He groaned and slapped himself on the forehead. 'Flipping Stupid Isles more likes—I is such a dinglebrain.'

'Nonsense,' I said. 'You is the greatest circus boss in the world and you're a brilliant teacher. I did things today that I never would have dreamed possible. If it was up to me, I probably would have run a mile before getting on that stage in front of everyone. But the thing is, even if the show had gone wrong, or people had laughed at me or even booed, it really wouldn't have mattered. When I got on that stage, I knew I wasn't the world's greatest circus star; it was just me, hiding behind a curly moustache, wobbling with nerves. But I remembered what you said—never forget to remember who you is—and, thanks to your brilliant teaching, I had the confidence to give it my best shot.'

Dr Smoothy nodded stylishly. 'As a seasoned performer of many years standing I say the kid's got a point. You two—' Zoltan coughed '—three were sensational today. That show was priceless. Why not stick around, Mr Baboomski, put on a show here? People will come from miles around, especially if there's koppletops in the interval! And in the school holidays, kids could come and learn circus skills.'

Mr Baboomski's moustache began to spin with excitement. 'I am liking this plan! But hold your horse.' His moustache slowed down to a gentle twirl. 'What about Zoltan? I is supposed to be getting her home to Ireland. I only ends up in Trefuggles because I is a dinglebrain that makes stupido mistake.' He looked at me and smiled sadly. 'But then something happens that I never can hope for: like Grandpappy with Pappy, and Pappy with me, I is getting the chance to share some circus learnings. Is true: sometimes a big pile of pootle can grow a beautiful flower.'

'Exactly! If I hadn't accidentally murdered Zoltan, we would never have met!'

Dr Smoothy's eyebrows shot up; Mum and Dad exchanged nervous glances. Then we all turned to Zoltan. She gazed back dreamily, tottered across the basket, gave me a soft butt in the stomach, then rested her shaggy head on my shoulder.

'**SKABOONKY**!' yelled Mr Baboomski. 'We is staying!'

'But are we?' I looked at Mum and Dad hopefully.

'The thing is,' said Mum with a sigh, 'my Special Project is finished now, it's time to head home, get back to normal.'

Dr Smoothy sniffed elegantly. 'I wonder if I might interest you in a new Special Project, heading up a conservation programme here in Trefuggle Bay? The scubbly is clearly a rare and beautiful fish that is in danger of dying out. It's our duty as citizens of Earth to protect it.'

'So we can stay?' I asked excitedly.

Mum smiled. 'Looks like it.'

Mr Baboomski cheerzed and Zoltan lowered a sleepy eyelid in my direction.

'Take us home, Dr Smoothy,' I said.

With a whoosh and a flutter the flipping great fruit drifted slowly across the bay, twirling gracefully back to the shore.

❧ THE END ❧

ABOUT THE AUTHOR ...

Richard Joyce has written two adult non-fiction books, the first about cricket—a sport he has an unhealthy obsession with—was nominated for the MCC and Cricket Society Book of the Year.

His first book for children is the product of an alphabetical negotiation: his family lobbied him for a pet, he offered them an ant, they badgered him for a badger, he countered with offers of a centipede, dust mite, earwig, and flea; in the end they settled on a story about a goat.

He lives in Hertfordshire with his wife and three children.

MORE WISE WORDS FROM BERTO BABOOMSKI

In life there is many ways to fight for what you needs—the important thing is to always use your head, especially when there is a monkey snoozing on it!

Life has a million minutes but only a few moments.

Why is mans always full of greedings and grabbings? Don't they see: in life, you only gets what you gives.

❦ GLOSSARY ❦
(as explained by Mr Baboomski)

ANGRY BATS: Circus peoples who is always swinging and swonging all over the shops.

GRUMPLISH: A mood like an old sock washed in a rainy cloud.

TRIPESTER: A people who is always sneakering around the place, cooking up pots of plots.

GOOTLE: Your rumbling tum. Here you finds food that you have eated and buttery flies when you is nervish.

BABUNSKA: A cheeky seat that you sits on when you is having some relaxings.

HONKER: You nose what I'm talking about.

SCUBBLY: a beautiful fishy, as silver as Miss Sylvie Starlight's pantaloons. Trusting me, you will yum your head off.

KOPPLETOP: Eatable Escorvian ball of fun (don't forget to remember to keep shushed up about the secret ingredient!).

SKABOONKY!: Betterer than the bestest!

CRAZLEPOPS: When you are so excited you is almost patoofling yourself!

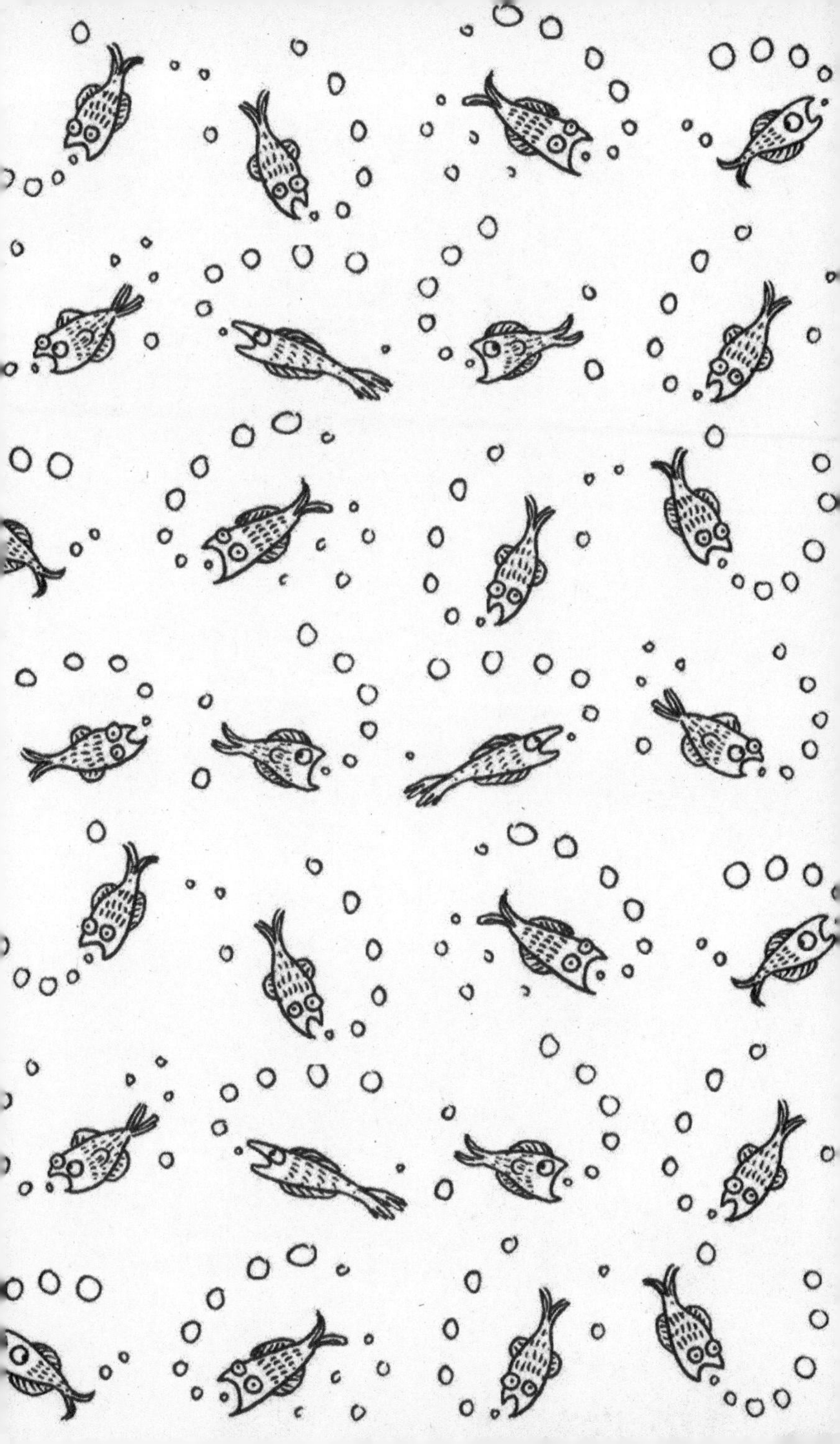